ADORE HER, MORE OF HER

DAISY & JACK, #2

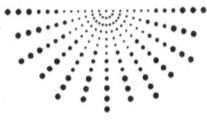

Z.L. ARKADIE

Z.L. ARKADIE BOOKS

ACKNOWLEDGMENTS

Thanks to the following:

    Edited by Red Adept Editing

    Cover Design by Z.L. Arkadie Books

For my fans, who have ventured with me this far. I've taken you on so many twists and turns that I know your head is spinning. I published the first book in the LOVE in 2013, which was Find Her, Keep Her (Daisy & Belmont, #1). I was so happy and satisfied with the story I had written back then, which starred a young woman of thirty-five.

And if you gathered anything from the LOVE in the USA series, then I hope it's this — you are never too old to be young enough to pursue the unique gifts you were born with. You have earth to till, love to acquire and true happiness on the horizon.

Here's to a happy life! This one is for you, and me. Much love, Z.

CHAPTER ONE

I balance on one foot and raise the other, pressing my heel against my thigh. As soon as I'm steady, I massage the sole of my foot. Yoga three times a week is paying off as far as perfecting my balance is concerned, but the bottoms of both my feet are killing me. I spent all day on them in the kitchen of Mes Fleurs Bakery today. Jeffrey and Rain—the senior bakers—and I were making special menu items for the final month of Christmas. Creating twenty-three different tasty desserts was easier in concept than in reality. From 8:00 a.m. all the way to 8:49 p.m., we whipped up croissants, éclairs, brioches, *religieuses*, madeleines, *macarons*, beignets, mille-feuilles, and a six-per-box assortment of petit fours. Baking was fun but exhausting. When I got home, I was surprised to see that Belmont hadn't arrived. He was supposed to be here five hours ago. It's our "both away" day. At least one of us is home with Ed, our son, four days of the week, and on the day both of us are out, Aunt Susan—my stepfather Joseph's sister—comes over to babysit. Her estate, where she grows acres of pomegranate trees, isn't that far away.

This morning, Belmont woke up earlier than I did, kissed me good-bye, and said he'd be home around five in the evening, depending on traffic. He drove from Montecito to San Francisco for a secured board meeting. I'm sure traffic leaving the city was a nightmare at around noon, but it should be all clear now. At any second, the headlights of his cream-colored SUV will be turning off the dark main road and onto our overly lit driveway.

"Hey, Daisy…"

Even though I know the speaker is not Belmont, I snap my face toward the doorway.

"You're leaving?" I ask Melvin, our chef for "both-away" days and special occasions.

"Yep. Kitchen's clean, and dinner's warming in the oven." His forehead wrinkles. "Jack hasn't made it yet?"

I shake my head. "No, he hasn't." There's no masking the concern in my tone.

Melvin looks past me and out the floor-to-ceiling windows. "It's raining pretty good."

I purse my lips into a tight smile and nod. Tears flood my ducts, but I'm determined to not release them. I have no idea why feelings of dread and sadness have suddenly overtaken me.

Melvin shows me a big, optimistic smile. "The roads are wet. Knowing Jack, he's taking it easy, making sure he makes it home safely."

I fold my arms and gaze out into the wet night. "I'm sure you're right."

"I am right," he says confidently. "So next week you won't need me, right?"

I quickly turn away from the glass and direct my manufactured expression of confidence at him. "Right. We'll be in Manhattan for all of next month."

Melvin snaps his fingers. "Dallas, right?"

"Huh?"

"Isn't Dallas Jack's New York chef?"

"Oh, yes."

"But who's the better chef, him or me?" He's grinning bigger than before.

I chuckle, welcoming the humor. "Well, you are, of course!"

He laughs. "Now, that's the spirit."

Now that the mood is lighter, Melvin waves good-bye. "Tell Jack I'm sorry I missed him."

"I will," I say.

We wave good-bye at each other one last time, and now I'm alone in this oversized room. My husband hasn't lost his taste for grandeur, no matter how hard I tried to bring out his more modest side. He does have one. But he also has a burning desire to make me happy. In his mind, a big home means he's a first-class provider.

A chill runs up my spine. I shudder and rub my bare arms. It's chilly in here, and the fact that I'm missing Belmont makes me feel how huge and impersonal this space is. I need to call him and see how close he is to home.

I find the remote on the built-in shelf above the fireplace and lower the shades over the glass windows. I turn off the lights, walk into the foyer, and climb the floating staircase. Belmont has realized that we're going to have to change the staircase out when Ed gets big enough to crawl and walk. These stairs are a child-emergency situation waiting to happen.

The smell of Ed's sweetness caresses my senses as I pass his bedroom. My office is on one side of his room, and Belmont's is on the other. I never pictured myself as a mother, even after I lost Joella, my first child. But I love being Ed's mother. I show him pictures from his sister's very short life every now and then, and every time he sees them, he smiles. Watching him smile and giggle at her wide eyes reminds me of how much I miss my brother Daniel.

I make it to my office. My cell phone is on the desk. I call Belmont. The line rings once and then drops. I grunt curiously and try again, and again. The same thing happens each time. I wonder where could he be? Maybe he left the office later than he intended. He has gotten stuck in emergency meetings before. He's also had to travel out of the country at the last minute before. However, he's always called and informed me of the change of plan. Then there's the third possibility.

I flop down in my desk chair and clench my phone in both hands. It was over a year ago when Belmont told me the truth about himself. We had just completed a session with our therapist, Dr. Calvet. It was one of those sessions that was filled with tears and hugs. Belmont admitted that he'd been hiding secrets from me that had been destroying him from the moment he looked into my eyes the first time on Martha's Vineyard. He said something stirred his soul when he saw the depth of my sorrow. We've sat through enough sessions with Dr. Calvet for me to know that from a very early age, he'd cultivated a deep desire to fix his mother's depression, which in turn made him want to fix everyone else's. This desire to fix all the pain in the world was also linked to his secret, one he could only disclose to me.

I clearly remember the night after that session. As soon as we signed off from our videoconference with Dr. Calvet, we decided to shower and climb in bed to talk. My mind raced with possibilities of what he needed to disclose. Did he have another wife and family? Was he ill? Was he in love with another woman? I had no idea.

Ed's soft sobs come through the baby monitor, and I put the phone back on my desk and rush into his room. Cell phones are not allowed near Ed because of the harmful radio waves. Ed is standing in the cradle, clutching the rails. His big, bright-hazel eyes and his smile stop me before I reach him. Gosh, he favors Belmont.

"Are you calling Mommy?" I say in a sweet voice reserved just for him.

He jumps excitedly and laughs. I rush over to him

and swoop him up into my arms. I sniff his sweet skin and kiss his soft cheek. Realizing that Ed only wakes up this early for a few reasons, I go right into mommy mode and change his diaper and feed him Melvin's special baby food, an avocado-and-sweet-potato blend. Once he's dry and full, I lay him back down in his bed and sit in the corner chair to read Peter Pan in a soothing voice until he falls asleep.

I HEAR A BABY GRUNTING. IT SOUNDS LIKE ED. I'M AT the tail end of a dream that's hard to forget. Belmont has just told me to never forget him before diving into a hot, boiling pit of molten lava. Now the child is moaning for *mum-mum*... I open my eyes. Daylight floods the space. I'm still in the corner chair in Ed's bedroom, and he's standing against the rail in his crib.

"Hey, sweetheart," I whisper and turn to look out the window. Sometimes when Belmont comes home late, he parks in the driveway in front of the door. I don't see his SUV out there, but that doesn't mean he isn't home. He must've parked in the garage. After seeing me asleep in the chair, he probably decided not to disturb me and instead go straight to bed. But other times, he hasn't hesitated to disturb me when I've fallen asleep in Ed's room.

I lift Ed out of his cradle. He's soaked, but I want to find Belmont before I change him. "Let's go get Daddy."

He rests his cheek on my chest beneath my collarbone. He too is ready for a big hug and kiss from his dad.

"Belmont," I call as I round the corner to our bedroom.

The bed is made. My eyes search the entire space.

"Belmont?" I call louder as I walk quickly to the bathroom. He's not in here.

I race frantically through the rooms upstairs, calling Belmont's name. I make it to his office. He's not there either. Ed squirms in my arms. His diaper is soaked, and he's been pretty patient so far. Torn, I sigh hard and rush back to Ed's bedroom to freshen him up, which includes taking off the soiled diaper, wiping his skin, powdering his bottom, and putting on a fresh diaper. I don't realize how shaky my hands are until I lay him down.

I take a deep breath to steady myself. "Mommy will be right back."

The corners of Ed's mouth turn down, his skin turns red, and he does something out of character—

he just bawls. I kiss him one more time and hurry out of the room. His cries are louder as I rush down the stairs.

"Belmont?" I call.

I search the kitchen, the west great room, the east family room, the two powder rooms, the full bathroom, the wet room, the garage, and the indoor swimming pool. My thoughts are all over the place. I'm sweating like crazy, and my heart's beating out of control.

"Ed." The baby isn't crying anymore.

I run up the stairs and into his room. He's biting his toes as he stares at the blue-butterfly mobile above his crib. He looks at me with amazed eyes. His smile broadens, and he goes back to making sounds at the mobile. I want to bend over and grab my knees to catch my breath, but I can't rest until I at least know where Belmont is. I go to my office and check my cell phone. I have no messages or missed calls from him.

I call him. This time I reach a recording that says the number is no longer in service. I try seven more times before calling Harold Doe and getting the same message. I get another shiver down my spine like the one I felt last night. I grab the edge of my desk and take deep breaths until the dread passes.

Now that I've gotten my bearings, I call Meg, Belmont's executive assistant.

"Lord & Lord Enterprises, Jack Lord's office," she says.

I press my hand on my chest and fall back in my chair. "Meg, this is Daisy."

"Good morning, Daisy." Her tone is sunny.

"Have you seen or heard from Belmont?"

"No, not yet, but he's not supposed to be in the office today."

That's right. It's his day to stay home with Ed.

"Did you see him yesterday?" I ask.

"Yes, I did."

I give a sigh of relief. "What time?"

"Um…" I hear her shuffling in the background. "He had a meeting with the board of directors at nine a.m., and that was it."

"Did he make that meeting?"

"I never received word that he didn't."

"Okay, but he should've come home directly afterward."

"He didn't make it home?"

Part of me wonders if I should tell the truth. I've been careful to not disclose too much of what I know about his business from the moment he told me the truth about himself. My husband used to be an agent for a secret security organization. He promised me that he's not as active with "the agency" as he used to be. These days, he's only called on for consultations and occasional training sessions with new recruits, which are becoming less and less frequent. He said this was because new leadership was shifting the focus toward new technology and away from men on the ground, which he thought was a bad idea. "Never sacrifice one for the other," he said.

"Daisy? Are you still there?" Meg asks.

I clear my throat and focus on the moment. "Yes, but…" I shake my head. "I'll call you later. Thank you for the information."

I can hear worry in her silence. "Okay, but let me know if you need anything."

"Sure thing." I hang up.

I sit back in my seat and think about what will be the right course of action to take at this point. One name comes to mind. I snatch my phone off the top of my desk and give that person a call.

CHAPTER TWO

THREE DAYS LATER

*M*aggie stands over Grey Lansing, who's sitting at a table that holds rows of screens and monitors. He's examining video taken from surveillance of San Francisco.

Maggie, who arrived two days ago with Grey, grunts and squeezes the bottom of her chin in a gesture of frustration. "Jack couldn't have just disappeared into thin air."

"But there's something strange going on here," Grey says.

"Yeah, like what?"

Grey is unsuccessful at trying to stifle a yawn. He's probably only slept about five of the last forty-eight hours.

"The video we're pulling doesn't seem authentic," he says.

Maggie grunts and moves closer to the screen to get a better look. My eyes are fixed on Grey, Maggie, and the screen, watching them as if they are part of a nightmare that I can't wake up from.

We're in a tiny room in the basement of our house. I never knew we had a basement. And the setup is pretty elaborate. Computers and monitors are mounted against a wall, which Maggie and Grey operate with ease. The only reason I'm standing here is because I demanded they let me stay. There's no way I would let them leave me out of the full process of finding my husband.

An image of a quarter of a billboard, which is mostly obstructed by trees, expands to at least four times its original size.

"Look at the date."

I blink my tired eyes to focus on the center of the billboard, where the date of June 18 of this year is faintly written next to leaves of the bushy tree. That was almost five and a half months ago.

Grey's fingers move rapidly across the keyboard. "Here's what I suspect."

Five images appear across two screens. It's really

difficult for my brain to process what I'm seeing, and usually I'm pretty swift.

"This is satellite footage from June 18, and the information on this billboard is the same as it is here. But look at this," he says.

Two side-by-side images are front and center. Maggie points to the one on the right. "That's from three days ago, and the other is from June 18?"

"Yep," Grey says.

He and Maggie look at each other as if they're speaking without words. My mind finally connects the dots. The video they've been studying for two days has been doctored.

Maggie quickly faces me and frowns. "Why don't you get some sleep, Dais?"

I shake my head adamantly. I'm too exhausted to include words with my gesture.

She sighs hard. "Then I'm going to have to insist that you leave."

"No." My voice trembles. "Why?"

"Because the less you know, the safer you are."

I blink my burning and tired eyes. "I'm so damn confused. How did it get dangerous all of a sudden?"

Suddenly, the entire computer system shuts off. We're very still in one long moment of silence.

"How did you access that satellite footage?" Maggie asks Grey.

"Not through the agency."

"Shit," Maggie says under her breath. "I wish you would've told me before you did that."

"Why?" Grey says, looking perplexed.

"Because they're not supposed to know you have the ability to get around them."

Grey groans as if he's just now realizing the magnitude of his mistake. Maggie looks toward the stairway. My mom and Susan are upstairs, taking care of Ed. Heloise arrived yesterday. Her emotions have fluctuated from being pissed at Belmont for not coming home to being afraid that something could've happened to him—like, maybe he accidentally drove off into the Pacific Ocean. I've been too out of sorts to defend my husband's honor against the idea that he just up and left Ed and me, and too frightened to even consider the possibility that his corpse could be trapped in his SUV at the bottom of the ocean.

Maggie pats Grey on the shoulder. "I'll be right back. Let's talk, Daisy." She starts up the stairs, confident that I will follow.

Maggie's very skilled at getting her way. I realize that I have to be at my sharpest when dealing with her in this capacity. My legs and arms are heavy, and I haven't been able to stop trembling for days. I haven't slept a wink. It's a serious job to drag myself up the steps. But there's no way I'm going to let her take advantage of my diminishing mental state and talk me out of being involved in the search for my husband.

At the top of the staircase, Maggie presses her hand against the wall. The plaster shifts to the right, and we walk into the mudroom. It's still unreal that we've just walked out of a secret room and into where I do the laundry. Belmont said he'd told me all of his secrets. Well, he didn't tell me this one.

Maggie touches me gently on the shoulder. "How about we get some sunshine?"

I face her empathetic smile. I know what she's doing. She's trying to convince me to give in to my grief. "Okay," I say in my most assertive voice.

We walk out onto the terrace at the back of the house and take seats at the patio table. I sit up straight and wait for whatever Maggie has to say.

"How much do you know about the agency?"

I frown. "So you think Belmont's..." I clear my throat because I don't want to say the words that will breathe life into what's going on right now. "His disappearance has something to do with that?"

"Just tell me what you know, Daisy, and I'll let you know what I think."

A burst of anger ignites within me. This is my husband we're talking about, the father of my son. She should disclose everything she knows because I deserve the truth—all of it. I close my eyes and take a few deep breaths.

"I know how you must feel, Dais. Believe me, I've already put myself in your shoes plus the ones I'm wearing." Maggie sets her hand on the table with her palm facing up. After a moment, I rest my hand on top of hers. I could use some human touch.

"Thank you," I barely say, choking back tears. I've calmed down somewhat. "So..." I sniff. "Should I start from the beginning?"

Maggie caresses my hand harder. "Please."

WHEN BELMONT AND I CLIMBED INTO BED AFTER OUR session with Dr. Calvet, he gathered me in his arms and asked if I could just hear him out. I agreed. He started with the day we met on Martha's Vineyard and the woman I noticed on the ferry. Back then, Belmont had said her name was Kara and that she was an ex-girlfriend. Kara was on the ferry out of

Woodshole with me. I'll never forget the way she stared at me during our trip across Vineyard Sound. Anyway, after that therapy session, Belmont revealed that the woman's name wasn't Kara and she'd never been his girlfriend. From that point forward, he began to tell me the most surreal story I'd ever heard.

My mother, Heloise, and my stepfather, Joseph, were suspected of operating a drug-and-prostitution ring.

When Belmont told me this, I jerked myself out of his arms and responded with a loud, "What?"

Belmont reminded me that I'd promised to remain silent until he finished. I took a moment to recover and decided to try one of the new strategies Dr. Calvet had equipped us with—listening to what Belmont was saying and not just waiting for my turn to respond. I agreed that I had given him my word, but instead of going back to cuddling, I sat up straight and listened to him diligently.

"Joseph's business partner…"

"Merrick Gold?" I said.

"Yes. He was the one operating the illegal rings."

"But he died. Wait. It was suicide, wasn't it?"

"That's how it was made to look."

A lump formed in my throat and in the pit of my

belly as one question came to mind. "Did you kill him?" I could barely get the words out.

"No," he said. But I'd been with Belmont long enough to know that if he thought the notion of him killing another human was ridiculous, the tone of his answer would've been more of an exclamation.

I scratched the back of my neck, remembering how far therapy had gotten me. One thing I was supposed to do was not hold in my questions so that they festered inside until they detonated in a nuclear-sized explosion.

"Have you ever killed anyone?" I asked.

Belmont swallowed hard and leaned back against the headboard. "May I finish, please? I'll answer your question at the end."

When I nodded, my head felt weightless. I already knew the answer.

He assured me that he hadn't been an active operative for "the agency" since he left Las Vegas, where he'd worked as a male escort for them.

"So that's why you were working as..." I cleared my throat. "A gigolo."

"I was undercover, but yes. Most prostitution rings are widespread. Girls were being shipped from Asia, Russia, and all over Europe. There were even plenty of abducted American girls."

I pressed my palm over my heart. "Wow."

Belmont extended both arms, beckoning me to come back to him. The initial shock of learning he was investigating my parents had worn off by then, so I crawled across the mattress and nestled myself securely in his embrace. He continued.

The criminal organization was sending prostitutes to Martha's Vineyard during high season. The agency asked him to take the case because he had planted some roots on the island and was pretty well known among locals. During our ferry ride, it was Kara's job to initiate "category 4" contact, which was to make me acknowledge her so that I would see the two of them together when I exited the ferry. Mission accomplished. I saw them, of course, and when Belmont stood at the edge of my table two days later with his sunny disposition, it didn't take long to remember that he was the guy who'd kissed the strange woman with platinum-blond hair. But he said that from the moment he looked into my eyes, which were windows to my deep sadness, he knew that I would mean more to him than his mission.

"But why follow me?" I asked.

The fact that I was traveling to Martha's Vineyard set off an alarm. I could've been the glue that tied my mom and Joseph to the racket. It didn't take long to figure out that I had nothing to do with the prostitution ring. The agency wasn't convinced, though.

My body went rigid. "So none of it was real, you and I?"

He kissed me delicately on the forehead. "All of it was real, babe."

I shook my head. "Please don't patronize me, Belmont."

He squeezed me tighter. "I'm not. When I first saw you, I noticed you were very attractive, more so in real life than in the images I'd studied."

I flinched. "You studied pictures of me?"

"Babe, this is not going the way I planned. I want to get through this before you react."

I sighed hard. "Well, this is hard to hear. I mean, it sounds like you did all this research on me. Which now makes sense! You knew so much about the articles I had written and…"

"But look where we are now. There's nothing phony about how we love each other and the way we love our son," he said.

"That is true," I said with a sigh. "Heck, I'm not even sure that if I knew the truth then, things would've turned out differently. I wanted to go fast with you—I needed to after what Maya and Adrian had done."

We ventured off on a discussion about how unsurprising it was that Maya and Adrian were divorced and entangled in a bitter custody battle, but Belmont quickly got us back on track.

An opportunity presented itself to exonerate Heloise Krantz after Maya and Adrian traveled all the way to Martha's Vineyard to explain their relationship to me but ended up exposing Belmont as a gigolo instead. I count that dinner as the worst meal of my life. After I told him I needed space to process what I'd learned, he didn't want me to be alone.

The agency set up a big sting operation to catch Merrick Gold and all partners involved in his illegal operations. Belmont didn't give particulars, only that they set up a half-a-billion-dollar bi-deal. Belmont explained that "bi-deal" meant prostitutes and drugs. All of Merrick's associates had to "shadow mark" the agreement—in other words, they had to call a number, and on the second ring, someone would answer, and the partners would say, "Seek."

Neither my mom nor my stepfather called. The agency didn't want to clear them until Belmont could get Heloise to travel to Martha's Vineyard and then engage in a brief interaction with

Merrick. The morning after my mom and I shared a night of bonding over wine for the first time ever—along with deep, honest, adult conversation—she ran into Merrick at the docks, waiting for the ferry. Merrick lied to her and said he was in town, visiting family. Of course, my mom questioned him to death. She thought it was strange he was on Martha's Vineyard, especially when he'd just been in Vancouver with Joseph and her the day before and never mentioned a turn-around trip to the island.

"How were you able to listen to their conversations?" I asked.

Belmont replied, "Technology."

From that one conversation, it was clear to the agency that at least Heloise wasn't involved. When she called Joseph to tell him about running into Merrick, and then Joseph called Merrick because he was worried Merrick was going to miss their meeting with some production partners early the next morning, my stepfather's name had been cleared as well.

We fell silent. After a while, Belmont said he would like to know how I felt about what he'd just disclosed.

"I'm trying to work it out."

"Okay," he said gently in my ear and gave me the time needed to figure out my emotions.

I twisted around to face him. "I mean, are you screwing with my head?"

"Have you ever known me to screw with your head?"

"You just told a whole story that included you screwing with my head and my life!"

Belmont remained silent and held me tighter as all sorts of emotions raced through me. My sense of betrayal gave way to confusion. Did his story mean he never really loved me? But then a strong wave of memories washed over my hurt. We had been through so much together. He and I had dedicated our lives to being together forever. That hadn't changed.

"I'm afraid, Belmont. I don't know what everything you're saying means for us right now. You could've kept that to yourself unless it affects the here and now. Does it?"

"I'm no longer an active operative."

"But what does that mean?"

"I can never leave the agency, but like I said, I'm only called upon for special assignments."

I pulled myself out of his embrace. "This is so surreal."

He shifted his gaze downward, giving me a moment to adjust.

"So again... have you ever killed anyone?"

"Yes."

I jerked my head up, surprised he didn't attempt a more diplomatic reply.

"But only to protect myself or others."

His hands were the first part of his body that my eyes gravitated toward. I reached out to take his right hand. His skin was warm, the palm clammy. From the very beginning of our relationship, touching his hands had been the best way to know what was really going on inside him. That night, Belmont was nervous even though his expression and body didn't show it.

Without my asking, he went on to tell me how he became associated with the agency. "Remember I told you I used to be involved with a woman in Hollywood?"

"Yes," I said. Way before we met, he'd been dating a woman while trying to make a go at an acting career in Hollywood. That woman, his lover, was able to secure him many auditions, and he bombed every single one of them. The woman suggested he put his true skills to work. She thought he was really good at using sex to make women believe he cared for them, even those who were as shrewd as she was. However, what really convinced her that he should trade Hollywood for Las Vegas was the result of a psychological test she had given him. One night, while lying in bed after making love, she dared him to take the exam. He took it, and the results showed that he had an extreme case of what was called "the superhero complex."

What Belmont couldn't tell me back when we first met on Martha's Vineyard was that when this woman suggested he go to Las Vegas and work as an escort, it was to work for the agency, focusing on drugs and the illegal trafficking of women, girls, and even boys to work as sex workers against their will. That was the superman complex at work: he was the sort of person who didn't mind killing to save lives.

"But how did you get to know Maya?" I asked.

He shifted uncomfortably and ran a hand down his face. "Right," he said with a sigh. "To be effective, I had to take on real clients. It was a soul-stealing job. Maya purchased my services once, but I always maintained discretion over choosing whether or not to service clients. I never..." His forehead crushed into a severe frown. "If there was something about a woman that made me feel she was too vulnerable to have what she was paying for, I would pass on the job and refund their fee. Actually, it made me kind of famous. I was the fucking prostitute who said no. The more I turned them down, the more they wanted me. Maya was no exception. She wanted to stay friends. One night, she came into town, and we had drinks."

"Don't say you were drunk, Belmont, because it's so cliché," I said, rolling my eyes.

"I was, though. I used to drink a lot back then."

"But how could you be a spy and a drunk?" I was about to apologize for my harsh tone before he responded.

"I was neither a spy nor a drunk." I remember how hard he sighed before saying, "Maya was attractive. I did give one night with her a go. But I could never find the desire to have sex outside of my client list. So we just made out, and…"

"She performed fellatio on you." Saying that made my blood boil. I hadn't known Belmont at the time, but just thinking about her mouth wrapped around his perfect instrument made me jealous.

Belmont grimaced at the wall. "Being a gigolo does something to a man. I had lost the desire to have sex until I saw you on the pier that day. Fucking unbridled lust—it came out of fucking nowhere. It overtook me."

As soon as he said that, he turned to face me with that look in his eyes. Belmont tugged me against him, drew me under him, and began to explore that unbridled lust he had for me.

MAGGIE SITS BACK IN HER SEAT AND LOOKS AT ME AS though she's reading each facial expression I'm making. I twist my mouth and look away uncomfortably.

"Jack told you a lot," she says.

"But he never told me this, and I've always wanted to know."

She narrows her eyes inquisitively.

"Who or what is the agency?" I ask.

"I can't answer that question for you." She lowers her voice. "Not here. Not now."

I bang my finger against the table. "My husband is missing. I feel like I've earned the fucking right to know."

She raises her eyebrows, more than likely stunned that I've used the F word. Finally, Maggie puts her hands up in surrender. "Listen. I agree, Dais. But I'm thinking about what Jack wants, and that is to keep you safe."

My jaw tightens as I glare at her. I'm processing her words, and the rational part of my brain understands them. So I close my eyes and take a deep breath to give reason a chance to overpower me. "Okay, then. I guess I understand. What next?" I'm barely audible.

Maggie frowns contemplatively. "Can I tell you something?" she whispers.

I'm just a hair more worried than I was a second ago, and I didn't think that was possible. I nod.

She leans in close again. "I'm scared."

My headache turns more severe. "Do you think the agency did something to him?"

She sits back in her chair. "I can't tell you anything more about them than I already have. But Jack's disappearance sure does point in their direction."

"Okay, so…" I want to form this question carefully. "Why did the whole setup in the basement power off?"

"I believe it's because Grey used it to make a query off the agency's system. Something tells me Jack had a fail-safe on his system."

"Why would he need a fail-safe for that?" A sudden thought comes to mind. "And what about you, Maggie? Are you part of this organization?"

"No," she says, shaking her head adamantly. "I only work directly for Jack."

"I'm confused." I'm sure it shows on my face.

"You're supposed to be confused. Like I said, I need you to back down for a while and trust me to fill you in when I deem it's safe to do that."

I toss my head back and moan. I want answers— many, many answers! I want my husband home right now. And if he isn't here, I want to know exactly where he is. Also, I don't want to feel like this. This issue of his disappearance has gotten bigger than the world we live in. I know he's missing. Maggie has been working for Belmont for a while, and he has been extremely confident in her capabilities, so I trust she has what it takes to make my universe warm and cozy again.

I bring my head forward. "All right. I trust you."

Maggie smiles tightly. "Thank you. Now, listen. You're going to have to report Jack's disappearance to the local authorities within twenty-four hours, but before that, I'm going to assemble an investigative team."

"Do you need anything from me, like funds?"

"Not a cent."

"Okay, but I want to be there every step of the

way. Is that possible?" My eyes are pleading with her to say yes.

Maggie opens her mouth, but then she closes it. After heaving a sigh, she says, "I've been in your shoes, and they're so tight they make your brain hurt. So yes, I don't think there's anything wrong with you accompanying me during the initial phase of the investigation."

Finally, I let out the breath I've been holding. "Thank you."

She stands, and I rise to meet her.

"I'll be back later. Get some rest and food, Daisy. You're going to need both in order to get through this with your sanity intact."

I fold my arms and nod.

She nods and starts to walk away.

"Wait," I say abruptly.

She turns and looks at me with a question in her eyes. "What is it?"

"Don't do anything that will make Abel mother-less or Vince wifeless. Okay?"

Maggie stares at me with her lips pressed together. Then she sniffs and walks over to kiss me on the forehead. We hug tightly. I would never be able to forgive myself if anything happened to her while searching for Belmont. *Never.*

CHAPTER THREE

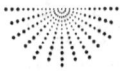

*M*aggie and Grey have left to locate another elaborate and secret system of computers and monitors like the one in our basement. I'm jittery from the lack of sleep and food, but I'm still not hungry even though I haven't eaten anything other than a small bag of trail mix and two energy bars since Thursday, which was the night Belmont went missing. However, I've drunk a lot of water and coffee. My steps are heavy but silent as I approach the great room. Heloise and Susan are having a conversation. I stop in my tracks when my mom says Belmont's name.

"I don't think he would do that," Susan says.

"Men get bored so easily, especially the ones like Jack Lord."

"But he loves his family."

"Then where the hell is he?" my mom snaps.

I clear my throat loud enough for them to know I'm here so they should zip it. Now that their conversation is over, I walk into the room. Susan and my mom look at me as if they're worried I've heard them. There was a time when my mom didn't care if she hurt my feelings or not. But ever since Ed has come along, she's worried that she would say or do something that would make me bar her from ever seeing him. I would never do that. My mom might be outspoken and entitled sometimes, especially as a big-time Hollywood executive who is so powerful that everybody literally wants to kiss her ass, but when it comes to me, her bite is toothless.

I look at Ed with heavy eyes. He's in my mom's arms, jumping his legs, excited to see me.

No matter how dreary our lives are right now, his excitement is the one thing that can make me momentarily see pink clouds, unicorns, and a light at the end of the tunnel. "Hi, sweetie," I say in a sweet voice.

Ed opens his arms for me, and I take him in my arms and hug him and kiss his delicate cheeks. He smells perfect and feels like the embodiment of hope.

"You haven't eaten a meal since I've been here," Susan says.

"I know. But I'm not hungry," I say.

"You should still eat."

"Daisy…" My mom stands and massages my shoulder. Not until she touches me do I realize that my trembling has gotten out of control. "How about you let me have Ed while you go upstairs and catch up on sleep?"

"And I'll bring something to eat. How does minestrone sound? I made a batch," Susan says.

I don't want to let go of Ed since he's all I have left of Belmont at the moment. But my throat is scratchy, my head feels as if I'm trying to breathe underwater, my eyes burn, and I can barely remain standing.

"Or a sandwich." Susan's voice sounds distant.

"Huh?"

"Instead of soup, I can bring you a sandwich."

I'm still not even close to being hungry, but I nod anyway. Susan scurries out as if she thinks she'd best hurry before I change my mind.

"Love you so much." I move in to kiss Ed again. But I halt, remembering that my throat doesn't feel too good because I haven't been taking care of myself in the last three days.

Z.L. ARKADIE

I give Ed back to my mom. He groans a little but settles comfortably into her arms. I've learned so much about little lives since he's come into the world. He must sense my distress, and now I'm more determined than ever to rest up so that I can get stronger. I'm no good to him or myself like this.

As I make my way upstairs, I kick myself for not making sure I got a few hours of sleep. I'm a few steps away from my bedroom when my cell phone rings in the pocket of my navy-blue hoodie. My heart constricts as I quickly take it out and study the face of the phone. My heart sinks. It's Jessica, one of the managers at the bakery. I can't talk business right now. I'm not available, so she's going to have to take the next step, which is to call Irving Vesper, the general manager. I silence my ringer and stop in the doorway of my bedroom. What's happening in my life is incomprehensible. I hate the sight of my made bed. When Belmont gets home and takes off his work clothes, he usually lays his crisp dress shirt over the bottom half of the chaise in the corner of our room. He did it the evening before he went missing, and I'm mad at myself for hanging up his shirt. If only I could see it lying there right now, I would pick it up and take in a deep whiff of his sweet, citrusy cologne. I would let myself indulge in the smell of his natural body oils and fantasize about how it feels to be wrapped in his strong arms. Tears fill my eyes. He just has to come home. It was fate that put us together. There's no other man in this world for me and no other woman in the world for him.

I look at our bed again. I'm so sad at the moment that I'm afraid to lie down on it. I used to have a pattern of sleeping away my sorrow. Even though I have the urge to do that, I don't have the luxury. First, I've been made aware that sleeping through the sorrow never solves a thing. The real healing begins when I'm on my feet and moving forward with life. Second, and most importantly, I have Ed to consider. I don't want the fact that his mother couldn't handle adversity to screw him up.

"I brought soup and a sandwich," Susan says.

I jump at the sound of her voice.

She's carrying a tray with the dishes on it along with a tall glass of ice water. "I didn't mean to startle you." She sweeps past me and sets the tray on the side of the bed where Belmont usually sleeps. "You should put on something more comfortable before you lie down."

I nod. And just like that, a tray takes the place of my husband in bed. "I will," I barely manage to say.

Susan squeezes my shoulder gently on the way out. I rub the top of her hand, showing that I appreciate her sympathy. When she's gone, I sit down and take a few bites of the roasted-turkey sandwich and minestrone. I force myself to eat more. I force my mind to remain free of thoughts of Belmont's disappearance as I eat. Thinking about nothing is extremely hard, but I battle to make it happen. When I'm done with most of the meal, I set the tray on the nightstand, drink the full glass of water, and go into the bathroom to change into a slip.

Once I'm out, I lower the electric shades and settle between the crisp linens of my bed. Anna and Isabella, our housecleaning team, must've changed them yesterday when they were here.

I play a little game with myself. "Dear God," I whisper.

Everything after that, I keep to myself. If he answers my plea, then I should be as happy as a lark when I wake up. I smile for the fourth time in three days. The three other times I've smiled have been while making myself show Ed a happy face.

I reach up to the switch on the wall beside the bed and turn off the lights. Then I toss and turn until I find a comfortable position, close my eyes, and force myself to drift off to sleep.

CHAPTER FOUR

*I*t's extra chilly this early morning as we stand in the subterranean downtown parking lot where Belmont was last seen getting out of his truck.

I'm staying out of the way as a private team led by a man Maggie introduced to me as Beck does his best to collect evidence. Beck is probably in his late fifties, with pure-white hair, specs, and a curious yet timid nature. I watch his every move. He's very thorough. Maggie explained that finding any evidence is like searching for a needle in a haystack, but it's better to try than do nothing at all.

Maggie is about five feet away. She's turning very slowly in a 360-degree circle, sometimes stopping to jot down notes on a small pad. Talk about a woman on top of her game. She's already directed collectors to a nearly concealed doorway that opens to a stairwell and shown them certain corners where someone could've lain in wait. My heart is still breaking moment by moment, but Maggie has the sort of control and pragmatism that I wish I possessed. Sometimes when I look at her, it's hard to believe she's the same young woman I met over four years ago. I remember the dinner Belmont gave to introduce me to his family and friends. Maggie was definitely nice to me, gave me a hug, and welcomed me to the family, and although I could read in her expression that she was concerned about how fast Belmont and I were moving, she tried her best to conceal it. And for the most part, she succeeded—I'm just very good at seeing beneath the surface. But so is Maggie, which is why by the end of that miserable dinner during which I'd dodged as many personal questions as I could, she gave me an honest hug and said, "I now know why you're with Jack." She had come to a new conclusion about the relationship between Belmont and me. I didn't get exactly what her epiphany was then, but I get it now. I was so destroyed before I met Belmont. My relationship with Adrian had been a subconscious effort to give up on true love, but I would've stayed in an inadequate relationship with that narcissistic jerk forever. Thank goodness he left me for my then best friend, Maya. I was also virtually estranged from my parents. I was living life without much enthusiasm or hope for the future. It took a while to admit this, but I was basically just waiting for my life to end so that I could join my brother in the afterlife. I believe Maggie saw that I was the perfect sort of broken puzzle that Belmont couldn't resist putting back together again.

I shove my cold fingers into my coat pockets. We've been out here for over three hours. I feel connected to Belmont here since this was the last spot Maggie and Grey have been able to accurately place him.

"Mrs. Lord, would you like to sit in the vehicle?" one of the forensic guys says.

I jump slightly and quickly turn to face him. I was so lost in my memories that I didn't see him approach me. He's pointing at the lone sedan parked across the driveway. The engine hasn't been turned on because of the exhaust fumes it would emit, but it's supposed to be well insulated, and there are blankets inside.

I shake my head. "I'm fine. Thanks for asking." I

bite down on my back teeth to keep them from chattering.

"We're almost done here anyway."

"Do you think you found anything useful?" My heart thumps with hope.

"This scene has been contaminated five times over, but we're not trying to prove guilt or innocence—we're looking for answers." He sniffs, hawks, and swallows. "And we're going to find many of those..."

"Let's bring it in," Beck calls.

The collector that I was talking to shuffles away to join Beck, Maggie, and another man, and they discuss something. I partly feel as if I should join them. Standing here feeling cold, sad, and lonely has made me indolent. I actually could've stayed home this morning and in the process made this whole ordeal a lot easier for Maggie. She could've slept in the city last night, woken up at one thirty in the morning, and arrived here before two o'clock. But instead, she slept at my house. We drove to Santa Barbara and took my plane to San Francisco. I did nothing to help them or Belmont, and it's time for that to stop.

Before I can reach the circle, they disperse. Beck nods and smiles tightly when he sees me. I'm tired of facing the pity in their eyes. I'm pretty sure they believe all of this has been for nothing. They think my husband has run off, probably with another woman. I take a deep breath, which allows oxygen to help me return to my senses. Maybe I'm just being paranoid.

Maggie and I reach each other and hug.

She squeezes me tighter. "That was productive, Dais. If there's something here, then you better believe we've collected it."

"Do you really think he didn't just leave me?" Shoot, I want to take that back even though, deep down inside, it is how I feel.

Maggie releases me and grips my shoulders. Once she's sure we're making steady eye contact, she says, "Don't ever think that."

I try to look away, but she shifts her head until she's captured my attention again. "This is above the both of us. I have no idea what happened to Jack, but what I am sure of is that I'm going to find out. Got it?"

"Yes." I can hardly speak past the ache that has risen from my heart and into my throat. I want to break down and cry again, but instead, I stand firm and strong like the pillar of a woman before me.

"Good. Now… you know what to do next?"

I close my lips tight to keep them from trembling as I nod.

She presses a button on the secure-line cell phone and hands it to me. I put the device to my ear. Maggie takes my free hand and holds it tightly.

I close my eyes as the phone rings. Finally, someone speaks. It's a woman. I'm so dreading hearing any voice that I can hardly make out her words. She stops speaking and waits for my reply.

"Yes, um, I have to report a missing person." Tears glaze my eyes, and by the time I give the woman the name of the missing person, they roll like a rapid stream.

Ten Hours Later

Earlier, I answered all the operator's questions. She asked me to drive to the San Francisco police station to file a report, but then Maggie took the phone and asked to be transferred to someone named Theodore Kelly. I think the operator gave her a little resistance, but Maggie firmly repeated, "Theo Kelly, now." After a few seconds of waiting, she was speaking to the man she'd asked for.

So now I'm at home, facing two detectives. One's a female, probably in her late twenties. She has dark-brown hair pulled into a bun that settles against the nape of her neck. I believe she said her name was Rosie Ruiz. She's doing most of the writing. Her partner, Dale Buchanan, has been asking most of the questions.

Maggie had to return to New York but promised to remain in close contact. Heloise and my stepfather, Joseph, are sitting beside me on the sofa. As soon as Joe heard the authorities were getting involved, he made a beeline for Montecito. He told my mom to make sure I didn't answer any questions before he arrived. He was a lawyer before he became a big-time producer. I swear all the TV he and Heloise make is starting to affect their sense of reality. For goodness' sake! I'm not trapped in a cheesy primetime crime series, but their behavior says otherwise. This is the second time Dale has asked when I last saw Belmont.

"She answered that question already, Detective," Joe says, peering over the top of his glasses as if he's just waiting for the officer to cross a line.

I raise my hand in an effort to get him to relax. I

don't mind answering the detective's questions. However, my mother and stepfather are unable to break out of fight mode.

"On the morning of November 30, my husband woke up before I did. It was around six in the morning, and he left for the office."

"In San Francisco?"

"Yes," my mom says bitingly.

"Yes," I say without the hostility.

"And there were no problems in your marriage?" Rosie Ruiz asks without looking up from her pad.

I shake my head adamantly. "Not one." My voice cracks.

She looks up. "Sorry, Mrs. Lord. I have to ask these questions."

"I understand," I say with a sigh.

"Well, I don't," my mom says. "My daughter is going through a lot here. You've asked her about her husband's business dealings and whether he has a life insurance policy. You know good and fucking well he has a life insurance policy. He's a rich man with a family."

Dale Buchanan sets hardened blue eyes on my mom. "Ma'am, do you want us to find your son-in-law or not?"

"Yes, I do, but you won't find him if you're questioning my daughter as though she's a suspect."

"Ma'am, these are just routine questions."

"Mom?" I shriek and rub my hands through my hair. I swear I'm on the verge of a nervous breakdown.

Heloise rolls her eyes and folds her arms defiantly. Unfortunately, she's not going to stop.

"Does your husband have a home office?" Dale Buchanan asks.

"Yes, he does," I say.

"Do you mind if we take a look around?"

"Yes," my mom says.

"No," I say.

"Yes, we mind." My mom's insistent. "Not without a search warrant."

I shake my hands frantically. "Mom, will you fucking stop!" I can't tell her this is only protocol and that Maggie has this entire situation under control. They're not going to arrest me. Whoever she called earlier knows my husband's secrets.

Heloise gasps, grabs her chest, and looks at me as if I slapped her in the face. She's never seen me like this before. Heck, I've never seen me like this before. She's driving me nuts.

"Yes, Officers, you may look around the office." I rise to my feet.

The two detectives look at each other as if they're trying to make sense of all that's going on here.

Joe stands too. "I'll show them the way." He winks at my mom.

I roll my eyes. These two are such a team. Basically, he's going upstairs to keep an eye on them.

Heloise stands while Joe and the detectives head upstairs.

"There's a baby upstairs sleeping, so keep the noise down," she calls sharply before they all disappear out of sight.

"Mom, what's wrong with you?" I ask once we're alone.

She wiggles her head as if she's just been slapped in the face. "I was thinking the same goddamn thing."

"I just want this over with."

"Your husband is missing, and they're going to investigate you, ma fleur."

"Then let them, because I have nothing to do with my husband's disappearance."

"Well, someone does," she snaps.

I open my mouth to respond, but as soon as I do, what my mom just said stuns me. "Then you believe he didn't run away from me? Just the other day you told Susan that's exactly what he did because he's a man." I'm breathing like a mad bull. I guess I was more pissed by her comment than I realized.

"I was just upset. I apologize if you heard that. I just needed to hear Susan say something to the contrary, and she did." She shakes her head continuously. "Jack Lord would never leave you if his life depended on it. No, no... that is not it." Her French accent returns slightly, which happens when she's not careful to control it. She shakes a finger. "Although I would not put dirty business past Jack Lord. There is something about him."

Of course my mom would pick up on his double life. She's very intuitive.

"There's nothing about him, Mom," I say to throw her off the scent.

She observes me with narrowed eyes. I coach myself to not look away or appear nervous. When her probing stare ends, I stifle a sigh of relief.

She shakes her finger toward the upstairs. "But those officers, I want them out of this house and out there finding Jack." She nudges her finger toward the door.

"They will. It's a process."

Ed cries a little through the baby monitor, and

my mom and I take off toward the stairs. When we reach the banister, she grabs me and hugs me tightly. Only now does it dawn on me that Belmont is just as much her family as he is mine.

"It's going to be okay, Mom," I say because I have no idea what else to say.

"I know this. I want you to cry in my arms. Now, cry."

She squeezes me tighter and kisses the side of my face. I take some deep breaths. This feels so ridiculous, but she's not letting go. Heloise has always smelled like magnolias, even when I was a little girl. Once, I fell off my skateboard in front of the house and hit my head on the ground. It hurt so badly that I cried like I never had before. My mom happened to be looking out the window. She ran out of the front door, scooped me up off the concrete, and held me tightly. The hug she's giving me feels like the one she gave on that day. The warmth of her body and the way she's repeating, "It's going to be okay, ma fleur," makes me break down and wail louder and harder than I have since this ordeal began.

CHAPTER FIVE

CHRISTMAS DAY

Snow filters down from the sky and covers Central Park's landscape. I stand at the window, drinking a hot cup of Colombian coffee. My life is still unfolding as if I'm trapped in a horrible nightmare. I had to leave our house in Montecito. Once the media caught wind of Belmont's disappearance, they swarmed the road in front of our property. At least twice a day, one of them would get bold enough to trespass and knock on my door or go looking through the windows. It was no longer safe for Ed and me, so I followed through with the plan Belmont and I made before he went missing, which was to move us to New York until things died down. Not only is this building secure, but Maggie and Vince live in the building next door as well.

So far, none of the evidence Buck's team collected has led to any solid suspects or clues to where my husband could be. Maggie has explained the meticulous way in which she's following up on each lead. At one time, she and Grey had permission to access the agency's mainframe, but not anymore. They are using backdoor methods, ones that could be very dangerous if they're discovered. I tried to talk Maggie out of taking that risk, especially since she has a son, but she's certain Grey's smarter than everyone else on the planet and he'll be able to work in secrecy and know when it's time to pull the curtain on their operation. Now is not that time. She also warned me that we can never discuss their activities either on the phone or in any of my houses.

"They're bugged," she said the day we went for a walk in Central Park. She'd even asked me to leave my cell phone at home. "But live as if you have no clue that they're listening. Can you do that, Dais?"

I nodded stiffly.

I'm looking at the park now. It's all frosted by wintery snow. The authorities haven't come up with any leads. I've been cooped up in this apartment for the last two weeks. Just because I left Montecito doesn't mean the press isn't hounding me. The day before yesterday, Detective Buchanan called to tell me that for now, my husband has been legally presumed dead.

"What does that mean exactly? Are you still looking for him?"

"We questioned Mr. Lord's colleagues. And I even tasked a search team to drag the Pacific Ocean. Never heard of a car and a man driving out of existence, but that's exactly what seems to have happened."

I could only respond with silence. Each day that Belmont is gone, my heart breaks a little more. I'm not getting better. I'm not missing him less.

"We're not giving up, Mrs. Lord," he said. "But a death certificate has been issued."

"It's only been twenty-four days. I'd be more comfortable if you'd continue the search. If money is what—"

"It's not me," he quickly said.

"Then who is it?"

"The orders rain down from above, and I just follow them."

My hands started to shake. I knew deep down in my heart that whoever was responsible for Belmont's disappearance had long and powerful arms that reached far and wide. So I swallowed my anger and frustration and pleasantly said good-bye.

Since I have no choice but to put one foot in front of the other and continue on with life, I'm forced to deal with not only my business, but also Belmont's. That's why instead of moving back to LA, I'm staying at our fairly new Midtown penthouse apartment, which Belmont says has the best park view in the city. The day after we closed on this place, Belmont and I stood where I'm standing now. It was spring in New York, the park's favorite time of year. The cherry blossoms had sprouted. The tulips and roses were at their best. The grass and trees were pure green. And the city dwellers never let a moment of enjoyment of this park go to waste.

"I think you like this place," Belmont said with his mouth close to my ear. His strong hand massaged the curve of my waist and burgeoning hard-on pressed against its usual spot—the top of my butt, right in the middle.

"I do," I said.

"You used to hate New York."

"I used to hate a lot of things."

"But never this." He smashed his full-blown erection deeper into the crack of my butt and then slid it upwards. He then moaned and nibbled my neck.

"No, never that," I said with a sigh.

My husband was a man with a slow hand, gently rubbing and pinching my nipples, sucking and kissing and biting my neck and collarbone. I closed my eyes and sucked air in between my teeth as his hand slid under my slip dress and up my thigh. My sex creamed, drenching my crotch.

His finger slid up and down my clit. "No panties," he whispered thickly.

I pinched my head against his chest, only seconds away from climaxing. Back and forth, back and forth he stimulated me. One sensation built upon the next while his teeth greedily clenched the skin of my neck so that he could suck it deep into his warm, wet mouth. I moaned. My legs shivered. The spring scene slowly left my sight as Belmont guided me around to face him. Our hooded gazes connected as his breath crashed against my nose and mine against his chin. It was like the pause before the action began, but the longer we stood looking at each other, the more my heart churned and fluttered. Belmont lifted his hands with his palms facing me. I pressed my palms against his, which were damp. That happened when he was fully aroused. It didn't take long to realize that we were filled with the same overpowering emotions. Our lips came together for a deep and tender kiss. It was as if love was an energy that emanated from our bodies and made our two hearts one.

"I love you," he said with such depth that my soul fluttered.

"I love you too."

We kissed. The next thing I knew, my legs were wrapped around his waist and he was carrying me into our new bedroom. He set me down on the bed. I took my dress by the hem, and Belmont helped me lift it over my head. Our eyes only momentarily lost connection. I remember feeling as if our love had become new again. He gradually guided me back down onto the bed. I parted my legs, and he ceremoniously entered my wetness. We made love like never before, kissing, hugging, and squeezing each other so tightly that we at times had to fight for breath.

My house phone rings, and I jump. Only those affiliated with the apartment building call that line. I run over to answer the call before the sound wakes Ed. We have to leave soon, but he doesn't do too well if his sleep is disrupted by a loud noise. I pick up the receiver before the third ring.

"This is Daisy," I say.

"Mrs. Lord. Just calling to let you know that you have a delivery downstairs."

I tilt my head and pause. "But today's Christmas. It's a holiday."

"Mrs. Lord. You have a delivery, and you should really come downstairs, and um... you should come see this."

"See this?"

"Um..."

I sigh wearily. "Are there cameras downstairs?"

"No, they haven't been here for a few days."

I grunt, wondering why those reporters suddenly lost interest in learning what I think happened to my missing billionaire husband.

"Okay, well..." Ed's soft cries arise out of the voice monitors. "I'll be down shortly."

I hurry to Ed's room. As usual, he's standing against the rail of his bed, smiling brightly.

I can't help but smile back. "You're up. Lovely." I pick him up and hold him high as he giggles. "Are you ready for Christmas at cousin Maggie's?" Just hearing Maggie's name makes him flap his arms excitedly.

I change his diaper and put a warm onesie on him before we go to see what sort of package is waiting for me. I take our private elevator down to the lobby. Bing Crosby singing "I'll Be Home for Christmas" enhances the environment along with the scent that mixes pine, cinnamon, and sugar cookies.

The bottoms of my slippers crack against the pristine floors. Suddenly, a line of red captures my attention on the opposite side of the front desk.

"Merry Christmas, Daisy baby," croons a group of grinning strangers wearing red Christmas sweaters, green elf tights, and hats. They break out in song —"Merry Christmas, darling."

A line of dancers files out from around the corner, twirling, kicking, and smiling their hearts out. Ed is tickled by the spectacle. I should be happy as long as he's having a ball, but more than anything, I'm confused. I turn to look at the staff standing behind the desk. There are about five of them, and they all seem amused. Maggie walks into the building. She can't be behind this, because she looks even more confused than I do.

Maggie kisses Ed and then me on the cheek. "What's this all about?" she says over the music.

The song sounds like it's about to come to an end.

"I have no idea."

"Ho, ho, ho!" a jolly voice sings. Bells chime. Ed is

still having the time of his life. I'm pretty agitated by the fanfare. Suddenly, a fat Santa rounds the corner. Two leggy elves in short skirts saunter in my direction alongside Santa. Now Ed moans and clings to me like a spider monkey.

"Well, you must be the lucky lady," he says in a jolly voice.

I check over my shoulder to make sure he's talking to me. He is. I can feel my frown deepening. "What's going on here?"

"Why, you, of course!" He laughs merrily. "I have a special gift for you."

Now that Santa's too close, Ed screams bloody murder and tries to climb up my shoulder to get away from him. Maggie takes him out of my arms, and he clings to her.

"Why are you here?" I annunciate so that he can understand I mean business.

He does that creepy laugh again, and Ed cries and tries to crawl around Maggie. Now I see that it's Santa's voice that's frightening him.

"You're the lucky wife of a very generous husband."

I slap a hand to my chest. Maggie and I look at each other as if we're about to lose our minds.

"Belmont. He's here?" I ask Santa.

Just for a second, Santa looks conflicted.

"My husband. Is he here with you?"

"Um… and since you've been a nice girl this year, here's…" He's singing the last word. I guess he figures it's better not to venture off script.

I follow his eyes to the revolving glass door. The glass is turning. My head is light, breaths shallow.

"Oh my God," Maggie whispers.

I think she's expecting Belmont as well. But a tall man in a pristine black suit enters through the revolving doors, holding a red box as if it's the royal crown.

Suddenly, I'm struck by a realization. Belmont isn't here, but he probably arranged this entire spectacle months ago. He did the same thing last year.

We spent last Christmas on Martha's Vineyard. He woke me up before the sun rose and convinced me to put on my house slippers and a plush robe, telling me the lights were off in the garage and he wanted me to hold a flashlight while he looked for the cover to Charlie's boat. He said Charlie had been asking if he'd seen it, and since Charlie and Angel were only a few hours away from arriving, Belmont wanted to make sure he had an answer for him before they arrived. I thought it was strange. He'd never woken me up to go help him look for something before. Even if the lights were out, Belmont always found a way to not bother me. I actually loved that he asked for my help that morning. I saw it as progress. He had always done so much for me, and helping him in the garage was the least I could do. I was still halfway sleepy, but once we made it to the garage, the lights flicked on, and a full choir burst into "We Wish You A Merry Christmas." I was so surprised and happy that I hugged and kissed him, cried, and sang along. At the end, we walked outside, and Santa, being pulled by a reindeer sleigh, presented me with a tiny red-foil box with a big gold bow on top. I opened it, and inside was a business card that had my name on it and the parking address where my personal airplane, the *Daisy*, was housed.

"You bought me an airplane?" I said, hardly able to believe I'd just said those words.

Of course, I didn't think I needed my own private mechanical bird, but Belmont convinced me that it was safe because it had all the latest and greatest technology, and he had the cabin designed with my tastes in mind. Next, he swooped me off my feet, carried me to his car, and drove me to the airport so that I could see it. My goodness—it was a sleek aircraft with a beautifully designed interior that had large, comfortable leather furniture and glossy wood tables and paneling. My therapy had included learning how to feel worthy enough to accept my husband's gifts of grandeur. Thank goodness I had made progress in that department, because now whenever I have to fly anywhere in the world, the *Daisy* is my main source of transportation.

So of course Belmont arranged this. The tall man opens the tiny box, and inside is the most beautiful diamond ring I've ever seen. I gasp in awe, and my heart constricts. I've never felt so lonely and heart-broken. I'm struggling to breathe and remain on my feet. I'm sobbing as everyone studies me. I can't stop myself even though I'm trying. Ed is crying. Elves, Santa Claus, the ring bearer in black, and Maggie's frustrated face are spinning. I try to focus on Ed, but...

"MRS. LORD, ARE YOU OKAY?"

I blink slowly until I can recognize the face that's above mine. It's Dino, the front-desk manager.

"The ambulance is on the way."

I sit up. "I'm fine."

"You should stay down," he says, although he moves back so that our faces don't collide.

I hear Ed crying his eyes out.

"Daisy!" Maggie calls.

I stand. The elves, Santa, and the ring bearer in black are gone. Maggie must've cleared the place out while I was unconscious.

"I'm better," I say as I make my way to her.

Ed reaches for me. I rush to him as though my life depends on it. In a way, it does. This is it. His father, my husband, has disappeared and perhaps will be gone forever. Today, I have to pull myself together. I can't faint or fade. My son's present and future are my responsibility. I take him from Maggie. Ed hangs onto me as though he knows I'm the only parent he has left.

"It's going to be fine, sweetheart," I say, patting him gently on the back. "We're going to be fine."

FOR THE PAST THREE CHRISTMASES, CHARLIE AND HIS guitar would lead us in a night full of carol singing and dancing. At some point, we would play charades and then end the night watching the most awful Christmas movie we could find, like *Santa and the Gremlin* or something. It would be early into the next morning before we'd yawn and say we'd had another great Christmas celebration. When Belmont and I went to bed, we would make love in honor of one more year spent together in love, fidelity, and happiness. He made me so happy. I can't believe he's not here to make me happy still.

It would be so easy to stay home today and cry in my bed. But I can't. This is Ed's first Christmas. Also, Maggie, Angel, and Charlie wouldn't let me. So we've decided to take the day minute by minute. Abel and Ed have already opened their presents. I made myself smile and sing, "Yay" while clapping. Abel's happiness at times feels infectious. He's such a different child from when he first came to live with Maggie and Vince. Like Belmont and me, they've figured out how to incorporate Abel into their busy lives. The fact that he's in school six hours out of the day helps.

As far as the adults are concerned, we left our gifts unwrapped and under our trees, vowing to open them only when Belmont comes back. Now it's time to eat, and we're seated around the table. The meal is almost the same as it was last year—glazed ham, rosemary pepper rib roast with hollandaise sauce, crispy roasted new and sweet potatoes, slow-cooked sugar-plum tomatoes with green beans and kale, roasted Brussels sprouts with pecans, and apricot parfait and butterscotch bananas with vanilla ice cream for dessert. Dinner and dessert were provided courtesy of Flip-Flam Catering. I take my first bite of roasted Brussels sprouts with pecans, and the robust flavors expand in my mouth. However, I can't fully enjoy the taste because of my —our—circumstances.

Charlie shifts abruptly in his seat. "Shit, Maggie. Where's Jack? And don't give me that 'it's classified' shit."

"Don't you think if I knew I would've said something by now?"

"You're awfully protective of Jack's secrets."

Maggie clenches the edge of the table and leans toward Charlie. "But not at Daisy's or even your expense." She nudges herself in the chest. "This is killing me too, Charlie."

Vince massages her shoulder. "It's true. She doesn't know anything."

Suddenly, I feel pretty uncomfortable. "Should we be—" I look up and swirl a finger around the room. I thought we had to be careful when it came to talking about Jack's disappearance.

"My place is safe," she says. "So we can talk about anything we want. And I do have something to say. I've been holding it in all day because I wanted us to have a good time with the kids." Her voice cracks.

Vince is now massaging the back of her neck, and it makes me miss how Belmont used to comfort me in the same way when I felt stressed and tense.

"I've been looking for Jack every single day, and…" Maggie gets up and goes to a drawer. Charlie, Angel, Vince, and I are very still as she takes out a square contraption with a screen. "I was able to securely get this video from Grey today." She sits down and looks at me with concern. "After what happened earlier, I questioned whether or not I should show this to you."

I feel my whole face frowning. I'm pretty irritated by what she said. "I need to see everything pertaining to my husband. I'll be fine, Maggie. What is it that you have?" My tone is stern.

She studies me for a moment and then nods. "You all will have to gather around me. And what you see—you'll have to act as if you have never seen it. Is everyone clear?"

Everyone says yes in his or her own way.

We gather around Maggie, and she plays the video. My heart stops at the sight of my husband getting out of his car, and it breaks at what has happened by the end.

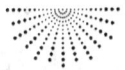

CHAPTER SIX

I flip from one side to the other. My shoulder and the back of my neck still ache, so I flop onto my back. When I last checked the time, it was 3:47 a.m. I had gone to bed just before midnight but hadn't been able to fall asleep. That video Maggie showed us hasn't stopped haunting me. Actually, Belmont never made it into the building. After he parked his SUV, Kara, the woman from Martha's Vineyard, stopped him. Maggie told me Kara's real name is Natasha. At first, Belmont appeared surprised to see her. Her smile was broader than the moon, and when she reached him, she whispered what looked like sweet nothings in his ear, and then they kissed—a deep, passionate kiss. My heart dropped to my feet. The two of them then got into Belmont's SUV and casually drove out of the parking structure. As soon as he made a right turn, his vehicle disappeared out of the feed.

Maggie cautioned me to not trust what my eyes saw. There were a few red flags in the footage. For one thing, Belmont looked genuinely surprised and annoyed when he first noticed the woman. Maggie and Grey tried a few methods to see if they could make out what she whispered in his ear, but the woman's lips barely moved. Maggie identified it as a tactic to conceal whatever she was saying.

"So he never made it to the board meeting?" I asked.

"No. I called Richard Wasserman and asked if he could confirm Jack's attendance. He said Jack contacted Gilbert Osprey and said he wouldn't make it because an emergency had arisen and he had to deal with it."

"What emergency?" I asked.

Maggie shrugged. "Jack didn't tell him. But he gave them permission to move forward with the meeting without him."

"None of this makes sense," I say, shaking my head.

"However, the video proves what I figured all along," Maggie said. "The agency took Jack."

That was Charlie and Angel's first time ever hearing about the agency. Maggie explained what she could and also warned them that the less they knew, the better. She reminded us once again that nothing we said should leave their apartment.

"How did you get ahold of that video?" Charlie asked.

Maggie explained how she has an associate who'd hacked a long-range foreign satellite. However, at the time that Jack drove out of the parking structure, most satellite cameras in the area had gone down for exactly two hours. When cameras went back online, there was no sign of Jack's SUV anywhere.

"So what does that mean? This *agency* took Jack? Why?" Charlie asked.

Maggie sighed, frustrated. "I don't know. But he may be back soon. You never know."

"May?" I asked.

Maggie looked at Vince with a bitter frown. He nodded. I could tell they'd already had a long discussion about what she'd just revealed.

Charlie pressed for more answers, but Maggie swore she had none to offer. I believed her.

There's a quiet knock on my bedroom door.

"Daisy? Are you asleep?" Angel asks softly.

She and Charlie are spending a few days here with me before returning to Los Angeles.

I sit up against the headboard. "I'm awake." I reach over toward the nightstand to turn on the lamp.

Angel tiptoes into my room and gets in bed beside me. "How are you?"

I shrug. "I don't know."

She watches me sympathetically for a moment. "Why don't you come back to LA with us? You and Ed need family right now."

For some reason, her words bounce off me as if I'm wearing armor. I know what I need right now. I press my lips together and smile tensely at Angel's expectant and hopeful expression.

"I can't run away from my future—the one without my husband."

"I know, but—"

I take one of her hands in mine. "I've been up all night thinking. On Tuesday, the board of directors is holding a meeting, and our lawyer, Frederick Holland, is supposed to attend on my behalf. But, um, I've been thinking."

"Thinking what?" Angel says eagerly.

"In Belmont's absence, he assigned me as his proxy in all matters."

She jerks her head. "But…"

"But what?"

"Well, Daisy, what do you know about lending your advice to a business enterprise of that magnitude?"

I'm slightly offended, but mostly, I'm aware of the rationality of her question.

"I'm just going to take it moment by moment. I need to be brave enough to at least attempt to do what my husband wanted. You know?"

Angel studies me with narrowed eyes and then sighs hard. "No, I don't know."

"Well, what about Charlie? What does he think?"

"Charlie is happy with the studio. He doesn't want anything to do with Lord & Lord Enterprise. Jack purchased Charlie's interest in their father's steel company years ago."

"Belmont made sure Charlie owned shares in the company."

Angel shakes her head emphatically. "We know this, but Charlie's really messed up over Jack's disappearance. I've never seen him like this before."

"Like what?" I'm extra curious about Charlie's reaction.

"He works all hours of the night and day. When he's home, he's on the phone, bugging Maggie about what she found. You know, he's driven out to your house in Montecito thirteen times, looking for any clues that will lead him to Jack. He swears Jack would never leave you."

I nod because I know that to be the truth.

"And tonight," she starts to say but then stops, remembering that nothing Maggie told us was to leave the apartment. "He just doesn't want anything to do with taking care of Jack's assets." She shrugs matter-of-factly. "He believes Jack will be back as soon as tomorrow. He's pretty heartbroken, you know?"

"Yeah, I know." My eyes venture down to Angel's five-month pregnant belly. It suddenly dawns on me that I'm not the only one who's going to go through a rough period of trying to adjust to the fact that my husband may never return. "Tell Charlie I'll handle Belmont's business and make sure it stays as strong tomorrow as it is today."

"Would you mind telling him that at breakfast? I think he needs to hear it from you."

Now I understand the main reason why Angel crept over to my room. She's a worried wife looking out for her distressed husband's best interest.

"No," I finally say, "I don't mind."

A slow smile forms on her lips. "You know, you're stronger than all of us, Daisy."

I want to believe her. "Well, you should've seen my big meltdown in the lobby this morning."

Her smile intensifies. "You're even strong enough to melt down when you need it the most."

I chuckle. "You are the queen of spinning."

She chuckles. "I wasn't spinning. It's true. I would be no good to anyone if Charlie went missing. And yet you've been out there with Maggie trying to find Jack."

I look around the room, acutely aware that I'm overly familiar with every piece of furniture and the dust that lies on top of it. "Not really. I've been holed up in this apartment for three weeks as a recluse."

"Yeah, but you had to because of the media. Everybody's speculating that it was foul play. But you've been cleared."

I bite my lower lip. I don't know how to respond to that. It has all been too much for me to bear, but not anymore. Soon I will face the media, Belmont's board of directors, and the strongest part of me I have yet to discover.

AFTER ANGEL RETURNED TO THEIR ROOM, I SLEPT A lot better, even if it was only for four hours. Angel slept through breakfast, but I assured Charlie that I would see to it that Belmont's businesses remain well-oiled machines. Of course, it would be through me personally voting on all matters pertaining to the board.

At first, Charlie frowned as if he wondered if I had the ability to read his mind, but then he said, "Thanks. Just let me know if you need me."

"I will," I said.

He nodded and then asked if I'd spoken to Jacques, my father, since... he couldn't complete the sentence. I told him I had, and like every other person I'd spoken to, he wanted me to abandon my life and come spend some time at Chateaux Mes Fleurs with him and Madeleine. Of course, I declined his offer. I wasn't ready to venture that far away from home. Like Charlie, I believed that Belmont was only moments away from returning to us.

Charlie and Angel left around noon to catch their flight back to Los Angeles. Angel wanted to stay to watch Ed for a few more days, but I assured her that Susan would be arriving later today and would be with us for at least two weeks.

Soon, I'll have to face the challenges of being a single parent while having what are sure to be demanding work responsibilities. Belmont and I had a system that worked for the both of us. At least I don't have to worry about Ed getting the short end of the stick for the next two weeks.

At the moment, Ed is catching up on sleep after an overstimulating holiday. Although the mood was somber, we worked very hard to make Christmas exciting for the kids. Before tending to business, I check on Ed one more time to make sure he's still sleeping peacefully. He is. A heavy feeling instantly comes over me as I walk to my office. Just because I have to handle business doesn't mean I want to. The phone in my office, which is connected to my cell phone, rings. I shuffle down the hallway to answer it.

"Daisy Lord," I say.

"Good afternoon, Daisy. This is Fred."

It's Belmont's lawyer. "Fred, I was just about to call you about tomorrow's board meeting."

"That's just why I'm calling you. We need to talk. Are you available this afternoon?"

"I can't leave. Ed is asleep."

"I can come to you."

"Oh. Okay. Then yes, I'm available."

He asks if I'll be free in an hour, and I say yes. I

look down at myself, still wearing my pearl-white pajama set. I go to the nearest bathroom to study my face in the mirror. The skin under my eyes is dark and puffy. Everything about me looks tired. My hair has been pulled up into the same top bun since the day Belmont went missing. Goodness, I haven't washed my hair in over three weeks. My mom's voice speaks in my head, telling me that if I want to be taken seriously, then it's my responsibility to appear as if I have my shit together. I rush to the bathroom, strip out of my nightclothes, and get into the shower. It only takes about fifteen minutes to wash my body and hair. Once I'm out, I dry off, brush through my curly wet mane, and twist it into a neat bun. I put on a pair of navy-blue bell-bottom trousers and a white V-neck sweater. The goal is to feel comfortable yet look casually powerful. After one last look in the mirror, I'm positive I've succeeded.

The house line rings as soon as I put on my slippers. I answer the call and give the front desk permission to allow Fred entrance to the elevator to our apartment.

I take a few seconds to gain my composure. Once my nerves are contained, I stroll confidently to the living room and unlock the elevator, which allows the car to open to our apartment.

There's a ding. The elevator doors slide open, and I'm facing a very tall gentleman with salt-and-pepper hair that makes his brown complexion glow.

"How are you this afternoon?" he asks.

I make myself smile. "Fine, thank you. And you?"

"Likewise."

I keep myself wrapped in this confidence I conjured and ask Fred to follow me to my office. During our walk, I recall everything I know about him. He's in his midsixties and has been an attorney for forty years. Belmont used to say as far as lawyers go, there's no one better than Fred. He's never been married, is childless, and has no commitments other than to his work. I've met him twice. The first time, I was eight months pregnant with Joella and hormonal as hell. He said the purpose of meeting me was to collect beneficiary information for Belmont's life insurance policy. He flew all the way from New York to Los Angeles to ask me a bunch of questions he could've asked over the telephone. It didn't take long to realize he was assessing me. He had a very sly method to his madness and began by starting a conversation about my famous parents, Heloise

Krantz and Jacques Blanchard. Before long, I was spilling my guts about how difficult it was growing up with them and how out of sheer defiance I'd worked to pay my own way through college and never took a dime from them. That was one of the strangest conversations with a lawyer I'd ever had. At the same time, I knew I had fallen into his trap. He wanted to know everything about me, and boy, did I tell him. Later that night, Belmont kissed me deeply and with a huge smile said, "I knew I married the right woman."

We laughed together after I told him how naked I felt after Fred's quasi-interrogation. "Heck, I even told him about Brian Ashby's lock of hair," I said.

"Who's Brian Ashby?" Belmont asked.

"One of my brother's friends. I had a crush on him. One night Daniel had a sleepover. My mom wouldn't let me sleep with six boys, so in the middle of the night, I snuck into their tent—which was pitched out on the lawn—with a pair of scissors. Brian had this ducktail on the back of his head. I cut it off, made a wish that one day he would notice me, and hid it between my mattresses."

"Did it work?"

"He's gay."

Belmont laughed his head off. He said he could just picture me sneaking across the lawn with scissors and looking like the most innocent person in the house when Brian woke up and discovered that the awful thing on the back of his head that he'd waited forever to grow was missing. Belmont called it a mullet.

"No, it was a ducktail," I said.

"What's the difference?"

I tilted my head to think about it. "I guess not much. They're both pretty uninspiring hairstyles."

Then Belmont went on show me a bunch of pictures of him wearing a mullet in the eighties, and I broke out pictures of me with purple, pink, and red hair.

The second time I came into contact with Fred was when he was handling all the legalese of getting Mes Fleur French Bakery off the ground. It was refreshing to have him working on my behalf. He had a staff that handled every single contract and license needed to start a business. My bakery was up and running in less than three months.

"Please have a seat," I say, guiding him into a chair at the round table for four.

"Thank you." Fred sits. He hasn't taken his eyes off me once. I'm pretty sure he's assessing me like he always does.

"You're welcome." I stand behind the chair across

the table. "By the way, can I get you anything? Coffee, tea, water?"

He raises a hand. "I'm fine. We should really get to it."

"Okay, then." I sigh and sit down.

"Jack has made you executor of his estate, and you're the sole beneficiary. I'm here to present you with options. If you liquidate…"

"No," I say emphatically. "My husband isn't dead unless I have a body to bury. So I want to keep everything he has intact. You understand?"

"I understand what you want, but I want you to be clear about the commitment that you're making. Jack left everything he owned to you, and he also dropped a lot of power into your hands."

"What do you mean?" I ask.

"Remember our first meeting?" he asks.

I smile slightly. "I'll never forget it."

His smile mirrors mine. "I was vetting you."

"Vetting me?"

He raises a finger and then opens his briefcase and takes out a small stack of papers, held together by a clip.

"Jack was aware that anything could happen to him at any moment. He was very assured that if something happened, then he would have you take his seat as CEO of Lord & Lord Enterprises."

My mouth drops open. "What? I mean, is this different than giving me the power to vote his proxy?"

"Very much different. He wants you to run his entire operation."

I feel the tension in my frowning eyebrows. "Me?"

"All you have to do is sign these." He hands me the stack of papers.

I hesitate but take them anyway.

"You don't have to do this," he says.

I start reading the legal jargon on the first page. I've read enough contracts to understand all of it.

"I have the bakery." I hold up two fingers. "Two of them now."

He nods calmly. "Yes, you do."

I look up from the forms. "What do you think I should do?"

He furrows his brow and then releases it. "It depends on what you want, Daisy. Taking over your husband's seat won't be easy. This contract is ironclad. Not one board member can oppose it if you agree to it."

I wait for him to say more, but he doesn't.

"You didn't answer my question. What do *you* think I should do?"

The phone rings. I'm inclined to ignore it, but the double chime means it's from the front desk.

"One moment, please," I say and answer the call.

The front desk tells me that Susan has arrived. I ask them to send her up and to let her know she can find me in my office.

I hang up the phone, retake my seat, and set my focus back on Fred.

"I believe you'll be able to do the job. But as I said, it will not be easy. There are three ambitious board members."

"And they are?" I ask.

"Todd Chandler, Richard Wasserman, and Gilbert Osprey."

"What makes them ambitious?"

"What makes any man ambitious? They want more."

I nod as I scratch the back of my neck. "I see."

"They'll test you. I've seen you get through tough times with Jack. He's made me aware that he shares a lot of his business with you."

"He does. I mean…" I feel a pinch of heartache. "He did."

He points at me. "Understand that you can't show them what you just showed me."

"What did I show you?"

"Your pain. Listen." He adjusts in his seat and leans toward me. "They're going to call you a bitch. They're going to try to prove you to be incompetent. When you make a mistake—and you will make a mistake—they're going to want to fillet you and then fry you in hot oil. They're going to claim you're a bad mother. You're going to have to fire more than half of the current employees, because that's how many are *not* loyal to your husband at this very moment."

"I don't care about any of that." My head is spinning because I think I've been holding my breath while listening to Fred's woeful soliloquy.

He sits back in his seat. "Then I don't think you should do it—I know you should."

A sigh of relief escapes me.

"Yoo-hoo, Daisy. I'm here," Susan sings.

Fred's gaze rises above my head, and before I can respond to Susan, he shoots to his feet.

I get up and race over to give her a hug. "Hey, Sus."

She smells good, as usual, like fresh pomegranate

and vanilla. It's a natural perfume that she makes herself.

"How are you, sweetheart?" She kisses me on the forehead.

"I'm fine. I'm in a meeting at the moment."

Susan raises her eyebrows at Fred.

"This is our lawyer, Fred. Fred, this is my aunt Susan."

He hesitates and then springs forward to shake her hand. Their eyes are locked. I'm pretty sure there's some attraction flowing between them. However, I could never believe they'd be drawn to each other. I mean, talk about apples and oranges. Fred is straight corporate, and Susan is a sixty-something hippie-slash- Mother Nature goddess. It took her years to warm up to Heloise, whom she once referred to as "a straight dragon bitch carved from the fires of Hollywood."

"Hello, Susan," Fred says.

"Hi, Fred." She's grinning like there's no tomorrow.

"Okay, well..." I say, rubbing the back of my neck. "We just have to finish up here."

Right on cue, Ed's crying blares through the monitor. I make a move to rush off and see to his needs, but Susan holds up a hand.

"Finish your meeting." She smiles deliberately at Fred. "It was nice meeting you."

Fred's awkward smile seems stuck on his lips. "Right. Same here."

I've never seen him so inarticulate.

Susan dashes off, calling Ed's name. I bet she couldn't wait to get here and hold the baby in her arms again.

Fred clears his throat. "So sign the contract, and I'll get them filed."

"Okay, then." I sit back down in front of the papers. The gravity of what I'm about to do seizes me. My declaration to make sure Belmont finds his life intact when he returns is no longer an oath. I'm making it happen.

I flip through the pages one by one. When I make it to the last page, I take a pen out of the metal holder in the middle of the table and put the tip of it at the beginning of the signature line.

"Shouldn't I read this before I sign?"

"Thirty-two f is an escape clause," Fred says.

That's the line above the signature that says I have thirty days to reassess, void, or amend the contract. I can't help but smile as tears rush to my eyes. This is how I know Belmont didn't just up and disappear of his own volition. Seeing to my comforts and needs, even though I resisted at every turn, was his lifelong goal.

I sign the contract. "I won't need to escape, and I'm pretty sure there's nothing tricky in those papers."

"No, there's nothing subversive in the contract as far as you're concerned." He winks.

"Thanks," I say, understanding that he means that anyone who opposes me won't be happy about what my husband has done.

I make a print copy and scan of the contract and hand it back to Fred, and he places it neatly in his briefcase.

"The meeting's at nine, but I want you to meet me in your office at eight."

I shake my head, confused. "My office?"

"Belmont's office."

"Oh. Right."

We shake hands.

"Enjoy your day," he says.

I'm about to say I will, but then another thought comes to mind. "What about my bakeries?"

"What you do with the bakery is up to you. Whatever you decide, just let me know, and I'll help you."

At first I'm confused, but then I get it. He's being

very careful not to overadvise me, and I think it has something to do with making sure I stand on my own two feet. As he said, this is going to be the most difficult task I've ever taken on. If I can't figure out what to do with two bakeries on my own, then I'm royally screwed when it comes to Lord & Lord Enterprises.

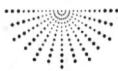

*a*fter Fred leaves, Susan and I take to the kitchen to warm up leftovers from last night's dinner. Ed is sitting in his high chair, making noises and shaking his arms, the way babies do, to the music box Charlie bought him for Christmas.

"How was your meeting?" Susan asks.

It takes a moment to realize I've been distracted by my thoughts while putting slices of the rosemary pepper roast in the oven.

"Oh, fine," I say.

"You don't look like you had a fine meeting. You look stressed."

I sigh as I close the oven door. "Well, these are going to be stressful times."

Susan stops spooning the potatoes into a pot.

"You do know that I'm willing to stay as long as you need me."

"I can't ask you to do that, Sus. You have your own life. I just have to find a nanny. One I can trust."

"That's ridiculous. I'm not going to put our sweetie in the hands of strangers. I said I will stay as long as you need me, and I mean it."

"But I'm going to be running my husband's business."

She jerks her head back. "Really?"

"Yeah."

"Oh." She appears speechless.

"That means I have no idea when I'll be leaving New York. I mean, Belmont could return tomorrow, and our lives could go back to normal, or it can take…" I press my lips together. I don't want to think about how long it will take before he comes back to me.

Susan nods tightly. "Well, don't worry. Between you, Heloise, and me, we'll figure out Ed's care. Because he's so special," she sings to him.

His bright smile does its job and lights up the room. Now that the roast is in the oven and the vegetables are warming, I go to pick him up and coo with him some more while Susan whips up a batch of fresh dinner rolls.

"By the way, what was going on between you and Fred?"

Susan stops in the middle of cracking an egg. "Who's Fred?"

"My lawyer," I say with surprise. I'm surprised she forgot him already.

"Oh… he doesn't want an old lady like me."

I stiffen. "What? You're about the same age."

She tilts her head curiously. "Is that so?"

I'm grinning, and I love it. "It is so."

"Humph." She grunts and goes back to making the bread.

I wonder what that meant. I guess she's not interested in him. Perhaps I read the whole situation wrong, which is why I choose to let it drop. Instead, I listen to Susan go on about planting more pomegranate trees. She's thinking about going into business manufacturing and selling her lotions.

"My decision would be a no-brainer if I were thirty years younger."

"Oh my God, Susan, the way you talk. You would think you were as old as Methuselah."

She turns to give me a definitive look. "Well, I am."

"No, you're not. You're sexy and earthy."

"I'm wrinkled and dry."

"You're aged and moist."

"Ha! Would you let me win this argument for once?"

I chuckle. "Never! Because I'm so right."

She laughs. "And that's one of a million reasons why I love you so much."

"I love you too."

We gaze at each other with warm smiles. Susan has been such a help in the last six months. We were never this close until after I gave birth to Ed. When Belmont and I first moved to Montecito, whenever I was on the telephone with my stepfather, he'd ask me if I'd reached out to Susan yet. I would say, "No, but I will soon." I meant to do it, but I was always too busy getting my business off the ground. Now that I think about it, I did an excellent job getting started. I have a full team of management and staff I can rely on. I'm pretty hands-on. I even work the registers at least three times a week. I'll sometimes bake, put in orders, and even work with Mindy to take inventory. Heck, I even clean toilets every now and then. Belmont used to cautiously say that sometimes I overcompensate for being unable to designate or ask for help. So I went back to work two months after having Ed. I was pumping and storing, so I didn't have to be present for Ed to be fed. But there were just some days when Belmont and I would get our lines crossed and I'd make him miss a big meeting or he'd make me miss one. Needless to say, our lives were discombobulated for a while, mostly for Belmont because he didn't want to be one of those dads who spent most of his time away from his children, but his commitments were a lot bigger than mine.

Then one day we found ourselves in a serious crisis. We both had important meetings the next morning that neither of us could cancel or reschedule. The decision took a lot of vacillating on my part. I didn't want to disturb Susan. I felt as if asking for her help was an imposition. But Belmont had to meet with out-of-country investors regarding permits to build a seaside resort in Costa Rica. I was interviewing Celia Knight for a position as my VP of product merchandising. So I forced myself to call Susan, who was happy to drive over and babysit Ed for a few hours. She has been Ed's primary babysitter ever since.

After Susan and I eat lunch, she takes Ed over to Maggie's to wade in their indoor swimming pool with Abel. I stay home and make a call to Celia and my general manager, Irving Vesper. I let them know that I'll be hands-off for a while. I don't know how long it will be. I also call Gabe Zenith, our accountant, and tell him the long story of how I'm taking over as CEO of Lord & Lord Enterprises. At first he's quite shocked, but then he tells me that he will be with me every step of the way, which is quite reassuring.

I'VE BEEN STARING AT THE CLOCK ON THE NIGHTSTAND for the last hour or so. The minutes have been passing slowly. I still can't sleep. Belmont is gone, a fact that still keeps me awake, but also, I'm extremely nervous about the board meeting that will commence four hours from now.

I can't sleep, so there's no use for me to keep trying. I kick the covers off and spring to my feet. First, I check on Ed again. I changed his diaper and fed him two hours ago, and now he's sound asleep. I go and take a shower and then spend time in my closet, selecting the perfect power suit. I put on a navy skirt and jacket, but I look more like the hostess than the woman in charge. I remember once hearing Heloise saying that being the head bitch in charge is more than a look—it's a state of mind. But the thought of having to become as tough as my mom to gain respect scares me. A black-blue pantsuit catches my attention. I purchased it at Burberry on Saint-Germain in Paris six years ago. The suit was such a stunning and elegant ensemble that I had to have it. When I bought it, I couldn't imagine an appropriate setting in which I could wear it. Heck, I forgot I owned it until now.

I find a crisp black shirt to wear under the jacket and the right kind of black patent-leather Mary Jane shoes. By the time I've finished tidying my hair and applying just enough makeup to wake up my tired complexion and eyes, it's time to call our car service.

I check on Ed on the way out. He's still in a deep sleep, but I lean over the rail of his bed to kiss him anyway. He stirs a little but doesn't wake up. How peaceful he looks. It makes me smile. I knock on Susan's door, and after a moment, it opens, and her face appears.

"I'm leaving. I checked on Ed. He's sleeping like a hibernating bear," I say.

She steps out of the room. "He always does."

I snicker lightly.

"You look wonderful," she says.

"That's the plan."

"Call me if you need me."

I hug her. "I will."

My cell phone buzzes. I have a text that my driver, Irwin, is waiting. We say our final good-byes, and I take the elevator to the garage.

Lord & Lord Enterprises is in Midtown. The building is too far to walk to, and although the drive is faster, it's littered with the worst kind of traffic. My nerves are on edge. As we stop and go and shuffle between cars, I close my eyes and try to meditate. This is all still so surreal. Good night! Sooner rather than later, I'm going to sit in front of the board of directors of my husband's company as the CEO. I feel so inadequate. I reconnect with my earlier thoughts about Heloise and what she said about how being the bitch in charge is a state of mind. *Bitch* has never been my style. I'm pretty sure I would suck at it. Goodness, if I have to become Cruella De Vil just to gain respect, I'm dead before I walk through the door. I take deeper breaths and envision myself running away from reality. I'm on a self-guided sub-Saharan tour, driving a dune buggy across the soft gold sand. The warm wind blows against my face. My life is perfect. I'm the only one who exists in this world.

"Mrs. Lord," Irwin says.

I open my eyes. The busy sidewalk is a dreadful

reminder that none of what I fantasized about is real. "Thanks, Irwin."

"You're welcome. And, um, sorry to hear about Jack."

My chest tightens as I look into his cautious eyes. Something tells me he may have realized he stuck his foot in his mouth.

"I'll call you when I'm ready," I barely say.

I think he says, "Okay," as I hurry to escape the back of the car. Unfortunately, the air isn't fresh enough to wipe the hurt from my heart. As I head into the building, I wonder if I'm making a mistake.

There's a lot of elevator traffic this morning. Belmont used to take a special executive elevator. It's two minutes before eight, and there's no way I'm going to make it to the seventy-fifth floor on time. I take a chance and dart toward the executive elevators. Once I'm there, a young guy in a baggy security uniform halts me.

I rifle through my purse, looking for my ID. "Sorry, I'm Mrs. Belmont Lord, and I have a meeting in two minutes."

"Executive badge, please?" he asks in a robotic tone.

"I don't have one yet, but I'll get one."

He points his thumb in the opposite direction.

"Sorry, you're going to have to take the regular elevators."

I look at how no one's waiting for the executive elevators. I could make my way up high in less than thirty seconds. This is my first challenge. Yeah, I'm frustrated as hell. I could go Heloise fully loaded, but I could also try out my own brand of get-what-the-hell-I-want.

"Sorry, but I'm the new CEO of Lord & Lord Enterprises. You heard of us, right? As a matter of fact, we own this building."

"Uh…" He examines me as if he's trying to figure out if I'm pulling his leg.

"If I'm late for this meeting, for which I now have only a minute to spare, I'm not going to be happy. And my being late will no longer be my fault. Therefore, you have two choices: let me take these elevators up, or send me back and make me late."

I look him dead in the eyes so he'll know that I mean business. I'm holding my breath, though, hoping he doesn't call my bluff. I would have to follow through on my threat, and I would hate to do that.

The security guard steps aside. He tilts his head toward the elevators. I walk over as fast as I can to push the button.

"That was impressive."

I jump, startled, and turn to my left. A gentleman about three inches taller than me is grinning. The elevator dings, and the doors open. I look past the gentleman and at the embarrassed security guard. I don't like what I just said, but I hate being late even more.

"After you," the guy says.

"Thanks." I enter. Talk about getting off on all the wrong feet this morning. I press the button for the seventy-fifth floor.

"I could've done that," the guy says, still grinning.

It's weird—I think he's being fresh with me. It's been so long since I've noticed a guy coming on to me. Perhaps he's just being nice.

"By the way, I'm Jetson Gordon. They call me Jet for short."

His hand is outstretched, and I shake it. "Daisy Lord."

"Nice to meet you, Daisy."

I tilt my head curiously. "Do I know you?"

He winks. "Do you?"

"Never seen you in my life. Do you know who I am?"

"Yes."

The doors open. After a long moment of

studying his smile, I step out of the elevator, and he exits behind me.

I turn to face him. "It seems as though you have the advantage here."

Jetson twists his wrist to check his watch. "We're going to be late, Daisy."

My mind processes what he just said. Who is this guy? Perhaps if I try hard enough, I'll remember his silver hair with a youthful face beneath and his keen grey eyes. This guy smiles a lot, which is different from any of Belmont's acquaintances. It's as if my husband only associated with the sourest people on the planet.

"You're here." Fred sounds relieved.

We both turn to see him standing in the doorway of Belmont's office.

Jetson tilts his head as if he's giving me permission to go first. I walk toward the office, still stuck in a fog of wonder. Once we're inside Belmont's office, Fred closes the door. Suddenly, the haze that surrounds me extends. I'm in my husband's domain. The scent of his skin moves through the air. I feel his presence, and I can't stop myself from closing my eyes and soaking it in.

"Daisy," Fred says carefully.

I raise my hand as I open my eyes. Dang it. I need

this moment. I'm still standing behind the two men, who have taken seats opposite the executive's chair.

"I've walked into this office at least six times before, and each time, his energy has overpowered me."

The two men remain silent as I take a moment to walk in front of the black-and-white blow-up shots of scenes from Yellowstone National Park. My husband loves nature. We were planning to spend Ed's first birthday camping in Yellowstone next year on June 23. Belmont wanted to show us the pristine lakes, dreamy waterfalls, and active geysers. I'm still hoping we can make that trip. I turn to face the other side of the office, where he has a wall-sized white bookcase. It's so tidy, holding his books on construction laws, work-project folders, and all other sorts of books and files that I'm sure are in their right places, according to Belmont, and positioned to make working easier.

I get my bearings and take a seat in his chair. As my butt presses against the leather, my carefully crafted composure wants to break, but I don't let it.

"Thank you for letting me do that," I say, choked up.

"Take as much time as you need," Fred says.

I can tell by the eager look in his eyes that he's

just being gracious. He was ready to start about forty-five seconds ago.

"I'm fine." I smile at the guy I just met in the elevator. "So why are we all gathered here?"

Fred introduces Jetson.

"We met on the elevator," I say.

"Mrs. Lord, Fred called me because he said you're going to need an ally. I didn't know your husband personally, but I've heard he runs a tight ship."

"And I need you as an ally because...?"

"Because Jack owns seventy-five percent of the shares in Lord & Lord Enterprises. The other twenty-five shares are owned by seven men who refused to give up their stake in Lord Steel. Half of the board of directors answers to those men."

I shrug. "I know all of that. And they can't get their hands on my husband's shares, which I now own, unless I sell them. I will never do that."

"There are ways of getting what they want, Daisy." Fred adjusts in his seat to lean closer to me. "Has Jack ever told you why he wanted to maintain full control of his enterprise?"

I nod, recalling how Belmont explained that he never wanted to be a captain who was forced to walk the plank of the mighty ship he built. "Yes. Many times."

"Jetson is Jack's kind of man. He's going to help you keep his banner floating on his ship."

I crack a tiny smile. "The mighty ship he built."

We grin at each other. I look at Jetson and sigh with relief. I feel as if half of my burden has been lifted.

"Okay, I guess we're a team," I say.

Fred hands me a two-page contract. "Then look this over and sign."

CHAPTER EIGHT

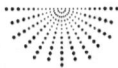

here are ten board members, and every single one of them looks either shocked or disappointed to see me. My heart is beating a mile a minute. I want to run out of this conference room as fast as I can. Fred has just announced that I'm the new CEO and Jetson Gordon is the president.

The sour-looking man that I recognize as Todd Chandler shoots his hand up in the air as if he's halting the craziness. "We have a president."

Fred glances at me. I feel as if I'm shrinking in my seat. "The CEO has appointed a new president."

"With all due respect, what does Mrs. Lord know about running this kind of company?" another board member asks.

I sort of detest how he's talking as though I'm not

Z.L. ARKADIE

in the room. The answer to his question is stuck at the back of my throat.

"Duncan." Fred shoots me a glance. "All that matters is Jack appointed her CEO of *his* company."

I understand the look he just gave me. Fred wants me to take note of this board member. I look at the agenda in front of me. The man's name is Duncan Winslow.

"There are shareholders, Fred, and they're going to be pretty dissatisfied."

"Then maybe it's time they sell. Mrs. Lord here is willing to buy."

Oh, gosh. My heart is beating faster.

Duncan Winslow sits back in his seat and scowls at me. I'm sweating under my suit. It's clear that I'm past the point of no return.

"The purpose of this meeting was to name Clyde Bowman as the interim CEO," the other woman in the room says.

I look down at my agenda. She must be Laura Altman, and Clyde Bowman is the company's CFO.

Laura looks at me with a tight smile. "Clyde is very well suited for the position, Mrs. Lord. It's what Jack would've wanted."

"He wanted me," I say, finally finding my voice.

Perhaps the words come because it's clear she's trying to placate me.

In one fell swoop, all eyes are pasted on me. I feel like taking a deep breath, but now is my time to set the tone of how it's going to be until my husband returns.

"To all of you at this table—I'm not going anywhere. I am now the CEO of this company. Mr. Jetson is our new president, and if any of the shareholders have a problem with either, as Fred has said, I'll be more than happy to buy their shares."

The room goes silent, and the tension is thick. Kirk Williams asks for Jetson's bio. Fred has it on hand and passes out a copy to each board member, and I promise to have Carlinda, Belmont's secretary, send a formal announcement of my new position— which will include Jetson's bio—to the company at large, including shareholders.

"That's not protocol at all," Laura Altman says.

I want to say, "It is now," but I'm very aware that I mustn't make it look as if I'm willing to engage in a catfight.

"Well, it is in this case," Fred says.

I fight the urge to grin.

"That went better than expected," Fred says.

Fred, Jetson, and I have gathered back in Belmont's office.

"Which means we really have to watch our backs," Jetson says.

"Absolutely," Fred replies.

I feel as if I'm in the middle of an exam that I'm hell-bent on passing. "I think we should call a company-wide meeting stat. I want everyone to know who's in charge. I want to get up-to-date on all the active projects, budgets, contracts, everything," I say, recalling all the talks I've had with Belmont regarding his work. The best way to stave off attacks that may come from a ravenous board of directors is to stay on top of things.

Jetson winks at me. "I'm already on it."

"How is that? We've just gone from the boardroom to my... I mean, Belmont's office."

"This is your office, Daisy. It's high time you start referring to it as such. How about we go out and have a cup of coffee and get acquainted with each other?"

I tilt my head thoughtfully to consider his invitation. "One second." I call Carlinda, who's probably at her desk, biting her nails, wondering if she's going to still have a job.

"Yes, Mrs. Lord," she says.

"Could you bring us a carafe of coffee and three cups?"

Jetson glances at Fred with raised eyebrows. Fred shows me two fingers as he picks up his briefcase off the floor and stands.

"Two cups," I say, amending my order.

"Yes, I can. Anything else?"

"Do they still provide morning bagels and fruit?"

"Yes, ma'am. I can just bring you some options."

"Thank you, Carlinda," I say and hang up. "Sorry, Jetson. It doesn't look good if we leave right after that board meeting. I remembered my husband provides a daily breakfast for all of his employees."

Jetson raises both of his hands. "No need to apologize. That was a good call."

I know it was. That board meeting has put me in fighting mode. Belmont was the best soldier I had, and he advocated for my happiness. Now it's my turn to do the same for him.

Carlinda has brought us a nice spread of an assortment of bagels, flavored cream cheeses,

Denver omelets with home fries, and fresh coffee with cream and sugar.

"Hungry, I see," Jetson says.

I've just taken another bite of a toasted cinnamon-and-raisin bagel with plain cream cheese. I put the bagel down on my plate. "Sorry, my appetite just returned with a vengeance."

"No, please continue. I enjoy watching a beautiful woman who's not afraid to eat."

I snicker. "Well... I'm not trying to please anyone, either."

He chuckles. "True."

I pick up a napkin and wipe my hands. "So where do we start?"

"How about how we'll work together? My role as president is to make sure all the departments are functioning optimally on a daily basis."

I touch my chest. "I'm sorry. Did I step on your toes earlier?"

"No, no, no," he says emphatically. "But I did sense that you might feel that it all falls on your shoulders. Well, it doesn't."

I feel confused again. "It always seemed as if my husband did everything for this company." I close my eyes to sigh with dread. "If I'm going to fill his shoes, then..."

"You can't."

I flinch as if his words just slapped me in the face.

"You're not Jack Lord. Hell, I'm not Jack Lord! Be yourself. I kind of think that's why he chose you to take his place."

I focus on Jetson's expression. Funny, I've been around him for the last three hours or so, and this is the first time I'm really clearly seeing him. He has the chiseled good looks of an older male model. Not only that, but there's a sort of sparkle in his eyes. It's as if he's a man who wakes up in the morning and chooses happiness over any other disposition. What a fascinating creature he is, although he looks like no one that my husband would ever associate with. It's the happy part that disqualifies him.

"And you've never met my husband?" I ask just to be clear.

"Never," he says. "Why do you ask?"

I shrug. "It's not that I don't believe you. It's just, I wonder why Fred thinks you'll be an asset to me."

"I've been an asset to him for a very long time. You can trust me, Mrs. Lord. All I want from you is what's on that contract."

"Twenty million a year. That's a hefty salary."

He smirks. "I'm worth every dollar."

It feels uncomfortable looking into his happy

eyes. I turn away, and the framed photo of Belmont and me cradling five-day-old Ed catches my attention.

"How long were you married?" Jetson asks.

Tears rush to my eyes. "Not long enough."

The silence lingers. Two loud claps take my attention away from the happy family in the photograph.

"I say we get down to business. But"—he points to my bagel—"I'll talk. You eat and listen."

I like the sound of that, so I pick up my bagel and get ready to listen.

CHAPTER NINE

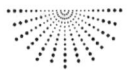

*E*ighteen days ago, I began my tenure as CEO of Lord & Lord Enterprises. I've met all the department heads and have introduced myself to every single worker. I never realized how large a company Belmont ran. There are three hundred twenty employees spread across the San Francisco and Manhattan offices. I've met most of management at one point or another in passing. They were smiling and very nice, hoping to make a good impression on me for the sake of scoring points with Belmont. However, now none of them have the ability to look me in the eye for long, and it seems as though they're avoiding me at all costs, even during moments like this.

I check the time on my watch—well, it's

Belmont's watch. I've been wearing it since the second day of working here. It makes me feel connected to him. This meeting has been in session for seventeen minutes. Hans Lowe is finishing up his report on the construction project in Monaco. Hans has already outlined all the hoops Belmont had to jump through to secure permits and licensing to build in a foreign country. He's also given his entire report without looking at me once. Instead, they're all speaking directly to Jetson, who has finally convinced me to call him Jet.

I have come to the conclusion that it doesn't matter if they pretend I'm not here. I am here, and I'm in charge. I read through the full report he passed out at the beginning of the meeting. I remember Belmont had to tap into a lot of his premium contacts in order to purchase prime real estate along the coast of Monaco. Some of those people were part of the agency world, so I'm not surprised the project has been stalled.

"Costa Rica is delayed." Eduardo Alvarez goes on about building inspections and unsigned permits.

I shuffle through all the handouts and find the one page on the Costa Rica project. I raise my hand. "Excuse me."

Eduardo glances in my direction. "We can't hire local workers without—"

"Daisy, did you have something to say?" Jet says.

I glare at Eduardo. Sometimes mini-Heloise gets agitated inside me and wants to break out with all guns blazing. "When did you learn about this project being stalled?"

His gaze bounces back and forth between Jet and me and then to someone who's sitting behind me and then to me again.

"Last week," he unenthusiastically says.

"Which day last week?"

He hesitates. "Wednesday."

"I don't understand why this is the first time I'm hearing about this."

He stifles a chuckle. I look around the room, and everyone appears to share his amusement. I want to shrink in my seat. They think I'm a laughingstock.

Jet glares at Eduardo. "What's so amusing?"

Eduardo shrugs. "Nothing."

"Why are we just hearing about this?"

"Because there was nothing we could do. We've been comparing notes around here. So far, eight construction projects have been halted because Jack hasn't been around."

"How in the hell did you know nothing could be done if you haven't told Daisy or me anything?"

"I just—"

Jet raises a hand to stop him from speaking. "Who else has halted projects?"

I count the raised hands. There are five of them, including Eduardo.

Lindsey Rather raises her hand slowly. "Construction on the West Manhattan project hasn't been halted yet, but yesterday we received a request from zoning. They want to inspect the site again."

"Jet, let's handle this immediately," I say.

Everyone watches me with confusion, but I don't let their looks hinder me. I open my calendar on my cell phone and let them know that I will have Carlinda schedule follow-up meetings with them, starting in two days. In front of everyone, I ask Jet if he's okay with ending the meeting. Without hesitation, he supports my decision. He definitely knows how to play this. It's clear he wants the entire company to know that there are no seeds of dissension to sow between him and me.

We wait until the room is clear and the door is closed to pick up where we left off.

"We need Fred's team on all these projects," I say.

"I'll send the list and see how fast he can get them rolling again," he says.

I smile, satisfied. "Thank you."

"You're welcome."

We're smiling at each other.

"You handled yourself pretty well." He winks at me.

"Ha!" I say, faintly amused. "I knew my propensity for not needing to be popular would pay off one day."

Jet lets out a loud laugh. "Well, you sure aren't popular, but just keep showing them why Mr. Lord put you in charge, and one day you'll wake up and you'll have all the respect you deserve."

Jet has the warmest gray eyes I've ever seen. He's more than handsome—he has a good soul. My curious gaze lands on his silky silver hair. I wonder how old he is. The company doesn't have personnel files on him because I'm paying his contract through Gabe Zenith.

"Forty-three," he says.

"Huh?" I'm snapped out of my indulgent stare.

"Are you wondering how old I am?"

I smirk. "Can you read my mind?"

"Sometimes."

Oh my goodness. I'm giggling as my gaze drops

to my lap. This is starting to feel an awful lot like flirting. So I scratch the back of my neck, take a deep breath, and regroup.

I shoot to my feet and thumb toward the doorway. "I have those budgets to look over."

He stands. "And I have construction sites to make active again."

Damn it. I'm smiling at him again. *It's okay to smile at him, isn't it?*

I start toward the door, and he picks up speed to beat me there. Jet opens the door so that I can pass. "Call me if you need anything."

"Will do." I keep my voice professional.

I'm pretty sure I'm being oversensitive. Not every guy who's nice to me wants to screw me. I press my lips together, smiling confidently as I make my way back to my office. Nope. He doesn't want me. Yes, we work well together. And yes, I can trust him.

APRIL 27, 2017—11:47 P.M.—LOS ANGELES

I'M TIRED AS HECK, BUT THIRTEEN HOURS AGO,

Charlie called and said that Angel's water had just broken. I arranged a flight on my airplane and flew to Los Angeles while Susan stayed behind with Ed. After I landed, a hired car drove me to the hospital. Angel was still in labor. The young nurse at the station told me they'd been waiting for me. I was put in a sterile gown and taken to Angel's room. I didn't need much guidance, because she could be heard moaning, crying, and screaming for those who could hear, "Help me, please!"

I was halfway to her room, so I picked up my pace and ran to her bedside. Angel bobbed her head from side to side on her pillow. He eyes were squeezed tight as she tried to endure the pain.

"Angel, ma fleur," I said.

Her eyes fluttered open, and when she saw me, she wailed, "I can't do this. It hurts too much."

I pressed my palm gently over her forehead. That was what Heloise did when I was in labor, and it made me feel a lot better.

"Shhh…" I whispered. "Everything's going to be okay."

"She didn't want the epidural," Charlie said.

I did a double take. He was hardly recognizable with his big, bushy beard, and the parts of his face I could see were very pale. The skin under his eyes was deep purple, and his already trim frame was thinner.

I wanted to ask if he was okay, but Angel let out an earsplitting scream, which shifted all my focus back to her. The tumultuous minutes crept by as Dr. Pennington guided her through the process. Then, at 10:23 p.m., Abigail Josephine Lord took her first breath of air.

It's now 11:47 p.m. The nurses have washed and swaddled Abigail and laid her in her tiny containment bed in the nursery. Our tiny little angel is sweet and sleeping so peacefully. I smile while crying on the inside as I remember my own beautiful flower, Joelle Marie. First Ed and now Abigail—both of their lives make me feel closer to the daughter I lost only three days after birthing her.

A hand rubs my left shoulder before Charlie appears to the right of me. He still looks as though he had been found after living on a deserted island for a year.

"Congratulations. She's a beautiful flower," I say.

"Yeah. I only wish Jack…" His voice is shaky.

"Me too." I rub his back as I turn to face him. Goodness, he looks like hell warmed over. "You don't look as though you're doing so well, Charlie."

He folds his arms. "I'm doing the best I can. You seem to be doing okay."

I'm not sure if he's judging me or complimenting me. "What do you mean?"

He glances at me and then sets his eyes back on his daughter. "You look like you're moving on, that's all."

I clench my lips. There are so many words inside me competing to let him have it. But then my eyes gravitate to Abigail. She doesn't need aunt and father arguing above her bed during her first few hours in the world.

"I'm going to forgive you for what you're insinuating, Charlie. I love Belmont. I miss him. I've gone to that office and have done my best for him every day, waiting, hoping, and just praying for his return."

He's silent, but I can feel his gaze on my cheek.

"Sorry, Dais," he says.

"You're forgiven."

I check the time on my watch again.

"Is that Jack's?" he asks.

"Yes, it's his."

His eyes turn glassier. After a moment, he looks off, shaking his head.

"What is it, Charlie?"

"I miss him. I don't know how long I can do this without him."

I crinkle my forehead. "Do what? Live?"

He shrugs.

"You're living now. You have a new daughter, and she needs you."

"I know that."

"Right. And you have a beautiful wife and a beautiful life. You've come a long way from the first time we met. Remember Martha's Vineyard?"

He snorts. "Don't remind me."

"Yes, I want to remind you. Take credit for your change. It wasn't Belmont's doing. You did it. You took an interest in yourself. So don't go backward—move forward. It's what your brother and the man that I love with every bit of my heart would want for you, and you know it."

I feel like I'm pleading with him to continue saving his own life.

Charlie's hand flies up to rub his neck. "You're right. Shit, you're right."

"I know it."

"Mr. Lord, your wife is awake." We both turn to the nurse who said that.

"Okay, I'm on my way." He looks at me. "Coming?"

I let my eyes indulge in our new beautiful flower one more time. "Yeah," I finally say. "I have to say good-bye."

"You're leaving?" He sounds surprised.

I face him again. "I have a meeting tomorrow at eleven. So yep, I have to fly back."

"Well, thanks for coming. Your being here meant a lot to all of us." He smiles. "Especially Abigail."

We turn in unison to dote on her.

"Look, Charlie! Her eyes are open!" I'm nearly clinging to the glass container, and so is Charlie.

"Hey, my love. It's Daddy," he says in a sweet voice.

I'm surprised. I've never heard Charlie do baby talk. It's good to hear. Happy that my little talk worked, I join him and dote on her some more.

I barely make my scheduled takeoff time. Being there for Abigail's birth has renewed me somehow. I still hope for Belmont's safe return, but if by chance the worst has happened, I'll be fine. Angel and Charlie have just gifted me one more new life to love completely and unconditionally, and that makes for a fulfilling future.

CHAPTER TEN

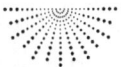

SEVEN MONTHS LATER

"There's Tante Daisy and Cousin Ed," Angel says in a high-pitched voice.

Angel and Abigail are on my computer screen. I feel guilty that I haven't been able to visit Abigail—we call her Josie, a derivative of her middle name—since the day she was born.

"Ciao, ma fleur. Ma belle, belle fleur," I say, wiggling my fingers at the screen. Josie shakes her arms excitedly. Ed is on my lap, laughing away. We've done this enough to where he and Josie not only recognize each other but have an on-screen relationship as well.

Ed, who is now one year old, starts talking about his book and something that's yellow, and even though she's just seven months old, Abigail squeals and speaks excitedly in nearly indecipherable words.

"She's so fast," Angel says. "And I love it!"

"I can't wait to hold her," I say.

Suddenly, the corners of Angel's mouth turn down. "Are you still working like a madwoman?"

I sigh as I ponder her question. "Truthfully, I don't know. I'm just going through the motions, and there are so many of them to go through. You know?"

Ed and Abigail are really communicating now, engrossed in their own conversation apart from ours.

"Listen." Angel takes a quick glance to the left and leans closer. "He's been gone for almost a year. I know you want to keep it all afloat for Jack, but..." She sighs gravely.

"I know... I never thought I'd say this, but I'm starting to think he's never going to come back."

"So if that's the case, then what does that mean for you?"

Ed tries to touch the screen. "No, sweetie," I say, guiding his hand back.

He says "no" and tries again. I turn him slightly so that we can see each other's eyes.

"Mommy said don't touch, right?" My voice is

stern but not harsh. It's the tone I use with him when I mean business.

He squeals and then buries his face in my chest.

"Come on. Talk to Josie before she says bye-bye."

Ed slowly takes his face off my chest. "Jos, Mommy say nnn…"

"Bravo," Angel says. "You're still so good with him."

"That's because it's my most important job. I can't neglect him. If I did, I'd be a double failure to Belmont."

Angel rolls her eyes. "Oh my God, Dais, that's extremely dramatic, especially for you. He's gone," she whispers emphatically.

"I know this."

"Then stop running two businesses while trying to raise your son alone."

"I'm not doing it alone. Susan's still here."

"And you hate New York. Just move back to Malibu."

"I can't."

"Okay, then, Montecito. Didn't Jack work from home and his San Francisco office?"

"Belmont didn't have a gang of Brutuses hovering over him with knives."

"Then let it go so they can't stab you in the back."

"That's easy for you to say." I set my jaw, and so does Angel. "Plus, Jet is a big help."

"Oh…" She sounds intrigued. "The silver fox?"

"The what?"

"I saw him on that interview you two did for Enterprise Now. He's hot, Daisy."

"Why are you telling me that?"

"Because, you know, you're going to have to think about moving on one day."

I feel my entire face crash into a severe frown. "I'm married. I love my husband. Jet and I are colleagues."

Her smile turns goofier. "But the way he looks at you."

"Let's change the subject, please. We have to talk about Papa's wedding."

"You're coming, aren't you?" She tilts her head and shakes it. "You better not back out, Daisy."

"I'm not. It's just that I can't fathom why Madeleine wants me to be her maid of honor. I don't even know her that well. You know her way better than I do. But it doesn't matter, because I can't. I have no time. Frankly, I think it's just Papa's way of getting me to come see him so that he can make sure I'm not falling to pieces."

Now I see it. Angel's eyes are wide and too innocent looking.

"Oh my goodness! Are you behind this?"

"What? No!" she says, feigning shock.

I sigh and wiggle my head. "Okay, I don't understand how you starred in so many plays, because you're *such* a bad actress."

She winks. "But I'm a great dancer."

"You tell Madeleine the jig is up. I cannot be her maid of honor. Heck, she didn't even ask me. She keeps sending me lists of duties and leaving messages telling me when she'll need me at the vineyard."

Angel laughs. "I know. She's a great partner in crime, isn't she? I told her exactly what time to call you."

"The times when I'm unable to answer my phone?"

She shoots her index finger at me. "Exactly!"

"You're so bad sometimes."

Strange, but I'm chuckling. Gosh, I love Angel so much. Sometimes I wish I'd met her long before I learned of her existence. But maybe not. My life has worked out the way it was supposed to. We became sisters just when I needed her most.

"Listen, can you please call Madeleine and tell

her it's over? I'm not going to be her matron of honor. You are."

"Okay," Angel says reluctantly. She tickles Abigail's belly. "We're going to stop messing with Tante Daisy so that she can work herself into an early grave and make Mommy unhappy forever."

I chuckle again. "Will you stop already? I have it all under control."

"Sure you do," she says as though she doesn't mean it.

"So how is Charlie holding up these days?" I ask in an effort to change the subject.

"Fine. A lot better. He's finally trimmed that hideous beard of his. He's getting rest and not working so much. But you know—he has his moments."

"Right," I say, getting a complete picture of what's going on between them. "Listen, can I ask you to do something?"

"Sure. Whatever you need."

"Stop pressuring him to forget his brother."

"What? I'm not doing that."

I tilt my head in a scolding manner.

"Okay, maybe a little."

"No way. More than a little. You've just given me the business about forgetting my husband and moving on. I know you very well, Angel. You're not giving Charlie the time he needs to deal with his brother's disappearance. Belmont was more of a father to him than his actual father. Charlie's not ready to concede to Belmont being gone forever, and frankly, I'm not either. I know you love us and want the best for us, but taking our time to get through this is the best we can do."

Angel groans as though it hurts to listen to my reasoning. "Okay... I understand, my older, wiser, and prettier sister."

She makes me laugh again. "I don't know about prettier but older and wiser certainly."

Angel laughs, and the kids join in with us. They have no idea what they're laughing about. We lead our babies through a round of saying good-bye to each other, then Angel and I say we love each other, she air kisses Ed, I air kiss Josie, and we say good night.

I get up and go give Ed a bath. Afterward, we sing and recite the alphabet together, and then I read him the story about the little engine that could. He responds very well to my expressive reading. During the day, Susan lets him sing and dance to *Barney* and *Sesame Street*. He can't wait to walk just so he could keep up with the friendly purple dinosaur.

As soon as Ed struggles to keep his eyes open, Susan and I lay him down for bed. The battle to stay awake and experience the world is on as he lies in bed and fights harder to keep his eyes open while sucking on his bottle.

"Strange thing happened today," Susan says.

"Oh yeah? What?"

"Well, two strange things. First, I was in your office, waxing the floor, and Ed was with me."

"Susan," I whine. "Estelle comes to clean twice a week, sometimes three times. You can relax and not clean here."

She touches herself gracefully on the chest. "Yes, but I'm better at it."

I crack a tiny smile. "You're just pickier. And can you please stop following her around the house, nitpicking? She's complained, you know."

She grunts and rolls her eyes. "I will respect your wishes, darling."

Gosh, I'm so relieved we don't have to get into a back-and-forth on this matter. "Thank you so much. You know, my mom has been asking me to send Ed to her for a couple of weeks—more like a month actually. But I can't be away from him that long. How about I let her keep him for two weeks so you can go home and..."

"Oh no. I don't need time away from Ed or you. But let me finish what I was saying."

"Oh, okay."

Ed has finally closed his eyes.

"We were in your office, and when he saw the photo of Jack, he pointed and said, 'Daddy.'" She whispers in order to not disturb Ed.

I grunt. I've never made a point of having Ed study Belmont's face. I didn't want him to have the stress of missing someone who wasn't here. But up until Belmont disappeared, the two of them were as thick as thieves. Belmont had worked overtime to not become the sort of father he'd had to live with.

"Well, that's good," I whisper.

Susan looks at me as if she doesn't believe me.

"What's the second thing?" I ask in order to abandon the subject of Ed reacting to a picture of his father. It's too heavy to deal with right now.

"Your lawyer, Fred, called."

"Oh, really? I met with Fred earlier this morning. He must've forgotten to tell me something. I'll call him now."

She takes hold of my shoulder before I can turn. "No, he wanted to talk to *me*."

I flinch, taken aback. "You?" Then I recall a few

things he said today that didn't seem odd then but do in hindsight.

"Why are you frowning, sweetheart?"

"Nothing. It's just, this morning he asked me all about Ed and how he's getting along. I told him that you're with him while I'm at the office, and then he started asking questions about how you're getting along in the city. Come to think of it, I ended up telling him that you were born and raised in LA but lived in Canada for twenty years with Don, your longtime partner. Goodness, he got me to tell him your whole story. I didn't even realize he was squeezing me for information about you until now." I shake my head. "Anyway, what did he want?"

"I ended up inviting him over for dinner tomorrow night. He's a lonely bachelor, and he might as well have dinner with us."

My eyes expand from a brief moment of panic. "Where? Here?"

"Well, yes. Do you object?"

The anxiety passes. Fred is such an intimidating person. I've never experienced him in warm-and-friendly company before. But as usual, there's a first time for everything. "No," I sincerely say.

Susan pats me on my shoulder. "You just let me know if you change your mind."

"I won't."

"Well, it doesn't look as if my news made you happy."

I take the frown off my lips and put on a smile. "Better?"

She narrows an eye. "Only barely."

I chuckle. "Just watch out, that's all. He knows how to make you confess crimes you can't even remember committing."

She laughs as she walks over to turn off the dim lights. "Your warning is duly noted. And... I also have a long list of tricks up my sleeve."

Susan and I part ways, laughing. Today, I was given a stack of contracts to review. After I shower and moisturize, I make a cup of mint green tea and climb into bed with the contracts. It's amazing how familiar I am with every single one I review. Belmont definitely shared a lot of his work with me.

Finally, I get to one that makes me grimace. "RT Creative." It's marked as "cancel" with no option for renewal.

There's no way this can be true. I remember Belmont going to bat for Robert when he ran up against East Coast competition. Robert and I have become pretty good friends after getting through the insanity that was Maggie and Vince's wedding. I know him pretty well. He used to be very careless when it came to business, but I remember Belmont being happy as a lark with RT Creative's work.

"I'll look into it tomorrow," I whisper and shuffle Robert's contract to the bottom of the stack.

There are two hundred and three contracts in total. By the time I get to the last one, I can barely keep my eyes open. I set them on top of the night-stand and welcome the sleep that is so elusive these days.

THIS MORNING, I'M AWAKENED BY A STEADY KNOCK ON the doorjamb of my bedroom. I sit up in bed. My hazy gaze rolls from Susan standing in the doorway to the clock on my nightstand.

"Shoot," I mutter and jump out of bed.

I thank Susan for waking me. Then I brush my teeth, wash my face, fix my hair, put on a light coat of makeup, and jump into a nice-fitting navy-blue wrap dress. Ed is still asleep, and I don't want to wake him. Instead of taking the elevator to the garage to be driven to the office, I walk out through the lobby, saying good morning to the desk staff and doorman on my way out, and join the New York sidewalk rat race.

My briefcase and I have been making the twenty-minute walk to and from work ever since I walked out of the office building and into a comfortable seventy-three degrees. It was clear at that point that winter had ended, so instead of calling Irwin to pick me up, I walked home. Spring was in the air. Trees were turning green again. Flowers were budding. People were out in droves, doing the bizarre things New Yorkers do like singing and dancing to the music in their heads, cursing and yelling at someone on their cell phones, or just cursing at someone who wasn't even there.

It's now late October, so it's turned nippy again, and on some mornings, it's rainy, but still I love to walk. Perhaps I'm finally becoming a regular New Yorker.

I'm standing on the corner, waiting for the light to change. The office is only a few blocks away. I'm itching to get there and discuss the contracts with Jet.

"Daisy," a man says very close to my ear.

I jump, startled, but before I can turn completely, he shoves a crumpled piece of paper into my palm.

My first instinct is to drop it, but as he walks past

me, my glare connects with his gaze. There's something about the look in his eyes that makes me crunch the paper in my grasp. The stranger and other pedestrians are halfway across the street. He looks homeless or something, but he's carrying himself as though he never made any contact with me whatsoever. The light turns red again, and I have to wait.

I'm pensive even after I reach my office. I flop down into my chair and unfold the piece of paper. An address is written on it.

"Good morning!" Jetson sings as he does each morning he appears in my doorway.

"Morning." I fold the paper and put it in my desk drawer.

"Have you read over the contracts?" he asks.

"Yep."

"Signed them?"

"Not yet. I have questions about why some of them are null."

He sits in the chair across from mine, staring at my face as though he's never seen it before.

I furrow my eyebrows and then release them. "What?"

"You look different this morning. More relaxed."

"Oh…" I open my briefcase and take out the

contracts. "That's because I actually got some solid sleep last night."

He sits back, shifting uncomfortably in his seat. I wonder what part of what I said could make him react that way.

"I want to say that it's been great working with you," he says. "I had my doubts you'd be able to keep up in the beginning."

I search through the contracts. "Same here." I find RT Creative and hand it to Jet. "This one. Why is it marked 'cancel'?"

He takes the contract. Our fingers brush slightly, and he pulls away very quickly. I've been ignoring this feeling I have that Jet is attracted to me. Of course, his feelings, if they exist, are one-sided. I'm still head over heels in love with my husband and don't foresee that changing anytime soon.

He grunts curiously as he reads over the contract. "I don't know. You'd have to ask Leonard. These are deals that were put together before I came on board."

"Right. But did you look at the files on them?"

"Sure did."

"And how did RT Creative look?"

"Looked good."

"Of course," I whisper as I get this sinking feeling

in the pit of my stomach. Something is *very off*. "I'll have them signed by the end of the day tomorrow."

Jet says, "That's fine."

Carlinda brings us breakfast, and we start our routine of going over the financials and agendas for this week's meeting. When we're done, I make the calls to the appropriate heads of departments to gather files containing paperwork or logs of all the future projects and any contracts that are in the pending-renewal and cancellation phases. I've been sitting in Belmont's chair long enough to have learned that everyone in this company wants me to remember that I'm not my husband. In order to receive anything, I have to wield a stick—sometimes a big stick and other times a shorter one. I spend up to two hours trying to get people on the phone who are eluding me. Carlinda has only collected files from the Accounts Department. Before my big stick and I head to Contracts and Projects, I call Vince to ask for Robert Tango's personal phone number. He gives it to me but tells me to wait ten minutes so he can text Robert and let him know I'll be calling.

"He never answers a call from a number he doesn't recognize," he says.

So to kill time, I walk over to Projects. As soon as Marney, Waite Miller's executive assistant, sees me, for some strange reason, she stands. Not too long ago, she told me over the phone that he was out of the office, but now I see him through the glass window, on the phone, with his feet on top of the desk.

Shoot. I'm seething. It's as if a switch has been turned on inside me. Marney says something to me as I walk past her desk. I strongly press my palm in front of her face to shut her the hell up. I feel the spirit of Heloise soaring inside me.

"Hang up the phone," I demand.

I'm pretty sure that if my look could kill, he'd be dead.

"Um, let me call you back." Waite listens to whatever the person on the other end says. He chuckles and says, "Later."

Now I'm more pissed than before because he doesn't even respect me enough to show a morsel of fear.

He shoots to his feet. "What's this about?"

I fight the urge to say that this is about him being fired. I'll eventually get around to that, but now is not the time.

"This is about you hopping to it when I say jump."

He grins mockingly, but I keep my *no bullshit* expression and posture.

"Do you understand?"

He throws his hands up as though he's giving up, although he still has that smug smile on his face. "What do you want, Daisy Lord?"

"You haven't answered me yet. Do you understand?" I raise my voice.

He looks past me, which is great because that means I'm making him uncomfortable. This is one of Heloise's most persuasive tactics. I don't take my eyes off him.

He shrugs. I still wait for him to speak.

"Sure, yeah, got it."

I turn to face Marney. "You received my request. I want those files now. I'll wait."

"Sure, okay." She darts over to a long file cabinet, pulling files one at a time from the list Carlinda had both emailed and hand delivered to her.

Finally, she's done pulling the files and hands them to me.

I look at the pile she's holding. "Next time, when I ask you to get something for me, my request is your first priority. Understand?"

Her nervous gaze shifts to Waite and then back to me. "Yes, Mrs. Lord."

I stroll confidently away. I want to take a deep breath of relief, but I can't. All eyes are on me as I pass cubicles and opened office doors. I turn to look inside Jet's office, and he gives me a thumbs-up. I wink at him. When I make it to Contracts, the executive assistant, Cecily, is out of breath as she tells me that she's already taken my request to Carlinda.

"It took me a while to pull everything. Sorry for the delay."

"Thank you," I say like the ice queen I have to be in order to get any respect around here. I continue my confident walk back to my office.

Not until I'm in the office, with all the files in hand and the door closed, am I able to sigh with relief. I really don't like being a bitch. I can always channel Heloise Krantz, but I don't like calling her forth to take names and kick ass.

After calming myself, I pull all the contracts and projects for RT Creative. From what I can gather, there's nothing indicating that his contract should be rescinded. So I call him.

"This is Robert," he answers on the first ring.

"Hi, Robert. This is Daisy."

"Hey, Daisy. First of all, I'm sorry to hear about your loss," he says.

I clear my throat as sadness pinches my heart and then releases. "Thank you."

"I got a text from Vince. What can I do for you?" He's back to sounding cheerful.

"I'm calling regarding your contract with us. Has Belmont ever spoken to you about not renewing?"

"No, never. As a matter of fact, we have two projects in the works and three on the horizon."

"Yes. I see that, which is interesting because I'm looking at a cancel request on your contract."

"Whoa…"

"Don't worry. I'm not canceling. As a matter of fact, we should extend so this doesn't happen again. I'm positive that's what Belmont wants. He was very happy with RT Creative."

We discuss getting together to hammer out his new contract. Robert makes a plan to fly out to New York next week. He'll bring Carter and hand deliver an invitation to their wedding, which will take place on New Year's Eve this year. His excitement about marrying Carter is refreshing. He just told me this cute story about how she snores in her sleep.

"Yeah, Belmont says the same about me, but I wonder how he can hear me over his own snoring."

Robert laughs. "By the way, I hear good things about how you're running Lord & Lord Enterprises."

I'm taken aback. "Is that so?"

"It came straight from Gabe's mouth, and he's not one for handing out undeserved compliments."

A picture of Gabe's inexpressive face comes to mind. "That's good to know." Suddenly, my gaze falls on the stack of initiated contracts. "Hey, I have a question for you."

"Ask away."

"Can I go down this list of names and you tell me if you recognize any of them?"

"Sure. Let's hear it."

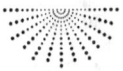

CHAPTER ELEVEN

I knew I wouldn't get through this process without facing some serious adversity. As soon as I mentioned Metropolis Architecture firm in Washington, DC, and Stuart Beatty, Robert recounted his tumultuous history with that firm. Right from the beginning of his story, it all came back to me. Metropolis was against Robert alongside the man Robert purchased his firm from to win a major project. Things got hairy. This Stuart Beatty guy even tried to use Robert's relationship with Carter against him. I remember Belmont working all day and all night to win the construction contract for the project so that he could hire the architecture firm of his choosing. That's how influential Lord & Lord Enterprises is in the commercial development industry, which makes what I faced today with the Contracts and Projects departments inexcusable.

I realize I have another major issue. Someone on the inside is working against Belmont's interests. I comb through every piece of paper on my desk, verifying my husband's signature, finding previous emails that correlate with the decisions made on the contracts and getting overly familiar with all active and future projects.

The sun has descended. I've already taken a break to call Susan and let her know I won't make the dinner with Fred as our special guest. However, I ask her to relay a message to him. Tomorrow, we have a lot of talking to do. Carlinda has already left for the day. She's not much of a worker bee. Belmont hardly spent any time in the New York office, so she had a lot of free time on her hands before I arrived.

"You're still here," Jet says.

I stop rubbing my eyes and yawn. "Yep."

He stands very still, studying me and then all the papers spread out on my desk. "What's going on?"

"Have you really studied all of these documents that I'm looking at?"

"What are those documents?"

"Contracts, proposals, accounts."

"Not like you're sitting there studying them."

"Well, you should've."

His smile wavers.

"I feel as if I'm being sabotaged," I say.

"Sabotaged?"

I point to the chair across from mine, gesturing for him to sit. He walks in carefully and takes a seat.

I go through the stack of faulty contracts. One by one, I show him why most of the ones that are marked to be canceled shouldn't be canceled. I also explain why the ones that are marked to be renewed should be canceled.

Jet blinks as though he's just been slapped in the face several times. I rub my eyes. It's dreadful not knowing whom to trust or not. So many questions run through my mind, and there's no way I'm too timid to ask them.

"Part of me thinks you couldn't have known. The other part is wondering how you could have missed it." I stop rubbing my eyes and search his expression for the answer to my question.

"If there's a conspiracy to weaken the operations of this company in any way, then rest assured I didn't know anything about it. I'm on your side, Daisy. I'm on this company's side."

The look in his eyes and the agitation on his face make me believe him.

"Okay," I say. "If it weren't for the cancellation of RT Creative's contract, my alarm probably wouldn't have sounded as loudly as it did."

Jet's eyes remain cold. "Thanks for bringing this to my attention."

I sit back in my seat and release a sigh of relief. "So we have to deal with this."

He sets his jaw and looks me straight in the eyes. "You did your job, and now it's time for me to do mine."

IT'S TOO LATE TO WALK HOME OR ASK ERNIE TO interrupt his evening to pick me up. I call a cab. The operator tells me the driver will be in front of the building in twenty minutes. I put all the files I studied today in one of my desk drawers and the contracts that I have signed, as well as the ones I won't sign, in my briefcase. I stand up to leave but then sit back down. I open the top drawer of my desk. There's the folded and crumpled paper the stranger shoved into my hand this morning. Could this be related to Belmont, or was he just another crazy man on the street? My heart is racing. I glance at the trash basket next to my desk, but tossing the paper in it doesn't feel like the right thing to do. Instead, I read the address yet again, neatly refold the paper, and take it with me.

I make it to the lobby of the building, but the cab that I called isn't in sight.

"Hey, Daisy," a familiar voice calls.

I quickly turn to look up the street. Jet stands on the driver's side of a sleek gray car. "Need a ride?"

I search in the direction I believe the cab should be coming from. "Um…" It sure would be nice to get home sooner rather than later. "Sure!"

"Then come on."

He sits behind the wheel, and I trot across the sidewalk and take the passenger seat.

"Thanks for the lift," I say as I buckle up.

"No problem. Where to?"

I look down at the sheet of paper in my hand. I can't have him take me all over creation. Plus, I'm not sure the address means anything yet. So I give Jet my address. It's late, I miss Ed, and I'm starving. I can't wait to dig into Susan's leftovers from her dinner with Fred. The thought of those two connecting over a meal makes me smile.

"You seem happier than you were in the office a while ago."

I chuckle. "No, I'm still pissed about the sabotage, but tonight, Fred's having dinner with my aunt."

"Oh yeah?" He sounds completely intrigued.

I look at the time on my watch. "Yeah, but I'm sure he's gone by now. It's going on ten o'clock."

Jet glances at my wrist. "Nice timepiece."

"Thanks. It belongs to my husband."

"Oh, okay," he says, nodding.

It's awkwardly silent between us.

"You still miss your husband?"

"More than you'll ever know."

He's silent again, but I feel his judgment in the air. I want to defend Belmont, let Jet know that my husband would never leave me of his own volition. Dead or alive, Belmont will never stop loving me.

"What about you? Are you married?" I ask to change the mood.

"What's that in your hand?" he asks simultaneously.

I shove the folded paper into a pocket of my briefcase. "It's nothing pertinent."

"Been divorced for three years."

"Huh?"

"You asked am I married?"

I'm flustered by how I so easily downplayed the mystery that I had been holding in my hand. "Right. Divorced? Sorry to hear that."

"Yeah... sometimes it doesn't work."

"Nope, sometimes it doesn't."

He shifts quickly forward and back in his seat. "I was wondering, though. Would you ever want to have dinner or something?"

I look at him with my mouth caught open. "Um..." I was not expecting him to say that at all.

"I thought I should put it out there. You're a beautiful lady, Daisy, on the inside and out. You're smart, and you have it all."

I think he's waiting for me to respond to his barrage of compliments. I swallow. "Um, thank you."

"Like I said, I just wanted to put it out there. But you're still in love with your husband. I understand, and I hope it works out for the best."

He stops at a light and studies me. Perhaps he's checking to see if I'm buying his BS. He doesn't hope for Belmont's return.

"Me too," I say.

"But if not, don't forget you have an admirer sitting right here in the car with you." He flashes his perfect smile.

My mind and heart are garbled with so many

thoughts and feelings. I have never considered Jet as a love interest. Inwardly, I have vowed to love Belmont and Belmont only until the day I die. That hasn't changed, and it never will.

The light turns green. I quickly turn away from his smile and gaze at my building, which is only a block away. After what happened between Dexter and me in Chicago, I want to be really careful about leading a man on. Dexter had it bad for me, and I don't want to relive that experience.

"Having no response can be a good thing," he says as the car pulls up to my building.

I turn to face him. The hope in his eyes makes me regret what I'm about to say. "I really appreciate your kind words, but I have no romantic feelings for anyone but my husband. And if I were you, I wouldn't wait for that to change."

I'm holding my breath as we peer into each other's eyes. I don't want to lose him as my business colleague, but if he's too infatuated with me to continue thereafter, then I'm very comfortable with continuing down this road without him.

"Then that's all I needed to hear," he says.

I nod stiffly. "Thanks," I barely say.

His lips make a slow smile. "Have a nice night, Daisy."

"You too."

I break eye contact and open my door.

"And if Fred is still there, tell him I said good job."

I tilt my head to one side. "Good job?"

"He's, um, expressed his interest in your aunt for a while."

"Oh," I say, intrigued.

"And don't worry. Tomorrow, I crack heads."

I blink, confused. "Crack heads?"

"I'm referring to the contracts."

"Oh. Yes. Thanks."

I smile at him, but he rips his gaze off me and faces forward. I finish exiting the car and close the door behind me. As soon as I'm out, Jet drives off. I know when I've broken a guy's heart. I've done it many times before.

When I step out of the elevator and into my apartment, the faint sound of Susan and Fred's laughter fills the air. He's still here. I check my watch again. It's 10:05. It sounds as though the dinner went well.

"Hello," I call, not too loudly just in case Ed's asleep.

"We're in the kitchen!"

I set my briefcase by the elevator. But then I hear Ed repeatedly say, "Mommy!"

As I walk into the kitchen, Fred is at the sink. The sleeves of his crisp white shirt are rolled up, and Ed is in his high chair with creamy green sauce and spaghetti pasted to his face.

"Well, look here," I sweetly say, shuffling toward Ed to give him and his messy face a big kiss.

He shoves another handful of whatever deliciousness Susan prepared into his mouth again as he giggles. When my lips meet his cheek, I feel as if kissing Ed is the one thing I've needed all day long.

"You're in time to join us for dessert," Susan says.

"Dessert?" I look at my watch. "Isn't it a little late for that?"

"It's never too late for dessert." Susan grins from ear to ear as she takes a cream pie out of the refrigerator.

My eyes dart over to Fred, who's just put the pot he was washing on the dish rack to dry. "Hi, Fred."

He faces me, grinning. "Evening."

"Did you enjoy dinner?" I'm beaming too.

"Very much so," he says, drying his hands with a towel.

"There's a dinner for you in the oven," Susan says, bouncing as she walks to the table like a happy fairy.

I take the plate out of the oven. She made ravioli and sautéed artichokes. There's also tomato-and-spinach salad sprinkled with asiago cheese and homemade pomegranate vinaigrette.

Of course, as soon as we all sit down, Ed goes quiet because he has fallen asleep in his pasta. After we check his mouth to make sure there's no food still in it, Susan volunteers to clean him and put him to bed.

"Did she tell you about her pomegranate trees?" I ask Fred now that we're alone.

"As a matter of fact, she did!" He's still grinning. It's evident she made an impression on him.

I smirk, still amused and fascinated by the two of them having dinner and getting along. "Did you get her to tell you her life story?"

He tilts his head back to laugh. "No, but I told her mine."

"Oh, really? Mind sharing?"

"Now, why would I do that?"

I study his sheepish grin. "So you like Susan."

He looks down at his lap shyly. "She's beautiful and interesting."

"Well, that's a good start."

Fred shifts uncomfortably in his seat. He clears his throat. "Why did you stay late at the office?"

I smirk. "Ah, the old bait and switch—I think."

He laughs. "No, it's called deflecting."

I laugh too.

His laugh simmers. "But if anything went wrong today, I'd like to know."

I fill him in quickly on the contracts issue. However, I let him know that Jet and I have identified the people who may have had a hand in the sabotage. Questioning and firing them is a task he will handle.

Fred narrows an eye contemplatively.

"What are you thinking?" I ask.

In walks Susan, and she's still glowing.

"Fred, I'll talk to you in the morning," I say.

Susan sits beside Fred. "Already talking business." She studies me and tilts her head. "What are you smiling about?"

"Nothing." I wink and take a bite of salad.

"Susan, you never finished explaining how to make a good bottle of pomegranate wine," Fred says.

She goes right into it as she cuts into what looks like her marble-cherry-cream cheesecake and places a piece on the dessert plate in front of Fred and then serves herself.

The deeper she goes into the wine-making process, the more questions Fred asks. They seem to speak to each other but occasionally look across the table at me. I think they're trying to include me.

"My ex-husband hated anything to do with nature. It was because he grew up on a farm," Susan says.

"Well, that's not how I am at all." Fred goes on to talk about how he lived on an apple orchard during the summer while studying at Cambridge.

Watching them genuinely enjoy each other's company reminds me of something. And once the memory grasps me, I drop my fork.

"I have to go." I quickly stand. Susan and Fred look at me as if they've done something wrong. "I'm sleepy, so I have to go to bed."

Fred says, "I should get going too. It's late."

I wave a hand for him to stay seated. "No, don't leave on my account."

He winks at Susan. "I'm not. Dinner tomorrow night?"

Susan's entire face lights up. "Yes, that would be nice. I'll walk you to the elevator."

They both stand. I remind Susan that she doesn't have to finish cleaning the kitchen because Estelle will be here in the morning. She gives me the look that says, *I can do a better job than her*, but agrees to leave the kitchen as it is.

When I make it back to the bedroom, I sit at the foot of the bed with my shoulders slumped.

Watching the connection bloom between Susan and Fred reminded me that tomorrow is Belmont's birthday. He'll be thirty-nine. My heart sinks. Tears roll fluidly from my eyes. For the first time since his disappearance, in this very moment, he feels lost to me forever.

CHAPTER TWELVE

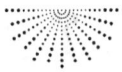

his morning, I call Irwin to pick me up. Last night, I slept in one of Belmont's crisp shirts for the first time and didn't take off his watch. It's as if the farther he slips away from me, the closer to him I seek to be. Ed had another long day yesterday, so he was sound asleep when I was ready to leave, and so was Susan.

I spend a few minutes looking for my briefcase before I remember I left it near the elevator. One look at the black-leather carrier, and I think about the note the strange man shoved in my hand yesterday. What am I afraid of? It wouldn't take much effort to at least drive to the address and see what's there. What if it was Belmont sending me a message? Maybe he's in a life-threatening situation and has to remain undercover. My mind entertains scenarios from bad spy movies. Each scene that plays through my head convinces me I'm off my rocker. What I fear most is that the man I encountered yesterday was just another eccentric roving the streets and occasionally including random people in his imaginary world.

Irwin is waiting for me in front of the garage exit as usual. I ask him to take me to the address on the paper.

"You got it," he says, and now we're on our way.

The city sidewalk scene passes by smoothly. Irwin is good at finding all the best streets to get us to our destination quicker. There are loads of people stamping the sidewalks. People are in such a hurry and focused on their journeys. Although I've warmed up to New York, I still miss Montecito and downtown Santa Barbara—the Spanish colonial architecture, beautiful beaches, and leisure walkers. Perhaps soon it will be time to go home.

Irwin double-parks the car next to a blue sedan. "This is it."

I look out the window, past a stack of trash bags on the sidewalk, to a row of old buildings. The garbage is way too close for comfort. I consult the page in my hand to remember which address I'm looking for. Found it. Lots of ladies in boots, yoga pants, and winter coats file into the building. I've been so distracted that I haven't realized how cold it is this morning. I want to tell Irwin thanks and he can drive me to the office now. However, I can't stop watching the ladies. There's something different about them. They're older and carry themselves with a certain air. This is the Upper East Side. Why would a nearly homeless man give me an address to this posh yoga studio on the Upper East Side? Just as I ask myself that question, I see a woman with dark hair pulled back into a ponytail and very pale skin. I recognize her immediately. It's Laura Altman, one of our board members. A car stops behind us and honks. Irwin doesn't budge. Thank goodness Laura doesn't turn to see what's up with all the traffic drama. New Yorkers can walk past a twenty-car pileup and not stop or turn to check out the scene. I'm the one who's antsy, but there's no driving off now. I decide to get out of the car, but just as I grasp the handle, another woman runs up the sidewalk. Her untied auburn hair swings across her back. She opens the door. I recognize her.

"Shoot." I release the handle, sit back in my seat, and close my eyes.

Irwin claps his hands. "Hot damn. Just got lucky."

The guy two cars in front of us pulls away from the curb, and Irwin takes the parking space.

Fortunately, he doesn't question my bizarre behavior. My cell phone rings in my briefcase. I take my phone out and answer it.

"Morning, Daisy. Jet here."

"I know," I say while keeping my eyes on the entrance to the yoga studio.

"Dude is making me nervous," Irwin says under his breath.

I turn to see who he's glaring at as Jet fills me in on the emergency meetings he's called with those we identified as the problems.

I gasp.

"I can include you if you prefer."

"No," I barely say while studying the man who shoved the address into my hand yesterday morning. I lower the window. "Handle it. I have to go." I end the call.

The man's gaze rises past the car and lands on the building. And now he walks away. I want to follow him, but he's moving so fast. Heavy traffic moves in both directions, so I can't run across the street. I turn back to the building.

"I'll be back." I scoot out of the backseat.

About seven minutes have passed since the yogis

filed in. If this is an hour-long class, they're only a quarter of the way into their workout. However, it felt as if the mysterious man was encouraging me to get out of my car and go inside. So that's what I do. The chill of the morning stabs me. Shoot, I forgot to put on my coat. But as soon as I'm in the building, I'm a little warmer. A steep and narrow staircase faces me. My steps are light, but my legs are trembling as I walk up. It's silent between the wainscoted walls and smells like eucalyptus oil. At the top of the stairway are elevators. A gold placard that reads East M Yoga—23rd Floor is above one of them. I get in and go up. I'm antsy, so I shake my shoulders and arms to ease the tension in my body. The only way to get through is to take it one second at a time. The doors open, and I exit the elevator. A light, new-age instrumental fills the hallway. I walk in the direction it comes from. The closer I get, the more I can hear the instructor talking her class through a breathing exercise. I tiptoe to the edge of a doorway and peek inside. About twenty women stand, breathing through warrior pose. I perform a quick scan of the room. I don't see Laura Altman or the familiar-looking woman who was the last to walk into the building.

I search the hallway, checking to see if there's

more to this place than the exercise room. There is. I walk cautiously toward a door with a Roof sign on it and open it. I go up a short set of steps and crack open the door. I can hear voices in the distance. Someone keeps repeating, "Hello?" as though they're on a call and nobody's answering. And then like a flash of light, I remember where I saw the woman. She was in the steak house with Belmont in Chicago. I saw her on the day I had my first in-person interview with Dexter Frampton. Belmont said they were work colleagues.

I edge the door open wider, hoping to get a view of the two women together. It doesn't take long to see what I'm looking for. I can't think of any reason why the two women would know each other. Is this what the strange man wanted me to see? I slowly close the door. The last thing I want them to see is me spying on them.

"Do you hear that?" one of them says. I think it's the woman I saw in Chicago. It doesn't sound like Laura Altman. I can feel them moving toward the door. I'm running but making sure my steps are light. I open and slam the door that leads to the yoga studio but keep hurrying down the stairway until I can pin myself against a wall where I can't be seen from above. My little plan works. The two women dash out onto the twenty-third floor, giving chase. I keep going down the stairs until I reach the bottom. I'm only slightly winded. Running down is a lot easier than running up, and I'm too excited to be too exhausted. Once I'm out of the building, I get into the backseat of the car.

"Let's go," I say to Irwin.

He glances at me with a wrinkled brow, probably wondering what that was all about. However, he does just as I say and pulls away from the curb. "To the office?"

I have to think fast. Who do I run to and tell what I saw? "Take me to Maggie and Vince's building." She'll know what to do with the information I'm about to pass on to her.

"Her name is Stacy Pruitt," Maggie says.

"Right. Now I remember." She sent me those emails of her and Belmont in sexual positions—totally doctored, of course.

We're sitting on stools at the island that separates Maggie's dining room from her kitchen. Her computer is on, and she's typing Stacy Pruitt into some sort of secure search engine. At least, that's what it looks like.

"And you said an unknown man gave you the address yesterday while you were waiting to cross the street and then showed up again at the address this morning?"

"Yes. Exactly." I'm wired.

Maggie frowns contemplatively. "Do you remember what time you left the building?"

"Somewhere between seven forty-five and eight in the morning."

Maggie punches a time range—seven o'clock to eight thirty—into her computer. She types my name. After a moment, right there on the screen is video of me walking up Fifty-Ninth Street and crossing Sixth Avenue. I'm waiting to cross Seventh Avenue when the man approaches.

"You can't see him stuff the address into my right hand, but he did."

"Yeah, that was a perfect exchange he made, and to a civilian at that." She sounds impressed as she cranes her neck forward to get a better look at the video. "And holy shit. I know him," she mumbles.

I put my face closer to the computer. "Who is he?"

"He has many names, and he's with the agency."

My stomach turns flips. "Why would someone who's with the agency send me to that yoga class so that I can see Stacy Pruitt and Laura Altman together?" Then I'm struck by a thought. "Unless…"

Maggie narrows an eye. "Unless?"

"Well, you've heard of Belmont's problems with the board members, haven't you?"

"They represent shareholders who refuse to sell him their shares. All the holdouts from Lord & Lord Steel. Out of respect for his father's memory, he decided to not use more *effective* tactics to make them comply."

"Right," I say. Her fiery expression catches me off guard. It's hard. It's mean. It's nothing like her natural Cinderella-like softness. "Anyway, I think there could be some kind of connection. So what do you think we should do?"

"I think I'm going to find answers."

I shake my head continuously. "There's no way you're going to do whatever you're thinking about doing without me."

"Dais…" She slips off the stool. "This is above your pay grade."

Suddenly, everything I've experienced in the last two days flashes before my eyes—the man stuffing the address into my hand, the contracts debacle, and me skulking up those stairs and discovering the connection between Laura Altman and Stacy Pruitt.

I hop off my chair, and now we stand face-to-face. "I don't think at this point you have a choice. I'm not going anywhere. Whatever you have to do, good, bad, or deadly, I will be right there with you." I cross my arms.

Maggie blows a hard sigh and then narrows her eyes to stare into mine. I suppose she's pondering what I just said. I remember her having the same position when Vince went missing right before their wedding and Belmont had to use his resources to find him. We're in the same boat.

"Okay," she says as though she's already regretting her decision. "But you do everything I tell you to do. Everything. Got it?"

I'm flooded with a sense of relief. I grab hold of her biceps, which, surprisingly, are rock hard. "I got it, and thank you," I say, and I mean it.

Maggie presses her lips together. Her toughness is dissipating right before my eyes. She grabs hold of me, and we hug tightly. Perhaps the man we both love will be at the other end of the rainbow.

CHAPTER THIRTEEN

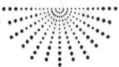

*T*his isn't Maggie's car. This car is smoky grey with very tinted windows and an elaborate display set up across the front panel. She's been having a conversation with a woman she calls Velma. This person is sending instructions to Grey Lansing, and he's feeding Maggie the information she needs. So here's what I've gathered. She knows exactly where to find Stacy Pruitt, who is on her radar. Maggie did question why the unnamed stranger who gave me the address didn't seek her out instead. It led her to conclude that she's being watched at what she called "a code-three level." She's now explaining that her apartment building has a disruptor signal installed, although she doesn't explain how it works, only that it allows her to feed false information to whomever is keeping tabs on her. The agency has brilliant people working for them but none nearly as genius as Grey's team.

"He has a team?" I ask as Maggie turns the car down an alley off of Eighteenth Street.

We're in Chelsea, slowly driving behind another row of tight-and-high apartment buildings. The woman Maggie called Velma has located Stacy. Apparently, she came to town just to have that meeting with Laura. And the fact that they met at the yoga studio when they did was no accident. The studio is Stacy and Laura's regular meeting place. They've been getting together quite often in the last few weeks, which probably has to do with the contracts issue. Maggie is only guessing at this point —she won't know more until she comes face-to-face with Stacy.

"Yes," Maggie says in answer to the question about Grey's team. She appears so unaffected by what's going on. The same scowl has been stuck on her face ever since we planted ourselves in the front seat of this car.

As I sit here trying to figure out when Maggie became this person, a small white courier truck drives toward us. Instinctively, I turn to look out the back window. It's so easy to get blocked into an alley in this city. Maggie peers at the truck until it stops. Two men in uniform hop out without even acknowledging we're here or that they've blocked us in and kept us from making an easy exit from this cramped alley.

I throw my hands up. "What in the world are they doing?"

"Stay here." Maggie rushes out before I can reply.

There's a loud click. The driver's-side door locks. My instincts tell me that I wouldn't be able to get out if I wanted. I keep looking through the rearview mirror, hoping no one blocks us in. Is stopping here even legal? I take a few breaths and try to remain calm. I have to keep my mind occupied. I look for my cell phone in my briefcase. Maybe I can call Susan and ask her how Ed is doing. It's a little chilly out, about fifty degrees. I'm not sure if today is Halloween Carnival in the park, but if Susan takes Ed out, I want to make sure he's appropriately bundled. She should put on his little bomber jacket with the thick faux-lamb's-wool lining and the knit cap that covers his ears and throat. That would keep him very warm. Now that I have my phone, I tap the screen to activate it, but nothing happens. I try again and again, and still, the screen is black.

"Shoot," I grumble under my breath.

This car must've deactivated my phone. So I'm antsy again. I keep looking out the back window and watching the door, waiting for either of those deliverymen to return to their truck or Maggie to come out of the building. I'm not even sure why she went in there. Is she planning on dragging Stacy Pruitt out kicking and screaming? Or maybe she's planning on squeezing her for answers while she's in there. If that's the case, I want to be there too! For a second, I'm inclined to open the door and head inside to look for her. I'm a little afraid to try, because I don't want to confirm my suspicion, which is that I'm locked in this car. Of course, this gives me something else to be antsy about. I drown out my frustration, clench my teeth, wring my hands, and just wait.

And then out of nowhere, I strike. I pull the door handle, and just as I thought, I am locked in this goddamn car. I feel like giving Maggie a piece of my mind when she gets back, but I remember what's at stake—finding out what happened to my husband and if he's dead or alive.

Finally, the rear door of the building opens. The two men from the truck are pushing a crate. They're behind their truck for a few seconds, and then they get in. The truck beeps as it backs up. I wonder how they're going to pull this off. However, my attention is diverted when Maggie casually walks out of the building. The lock to the car door clicks, and she's back behind the steering wheel.

"What was that all about?" My frown is so severe that my temples ache.

Maggie glances at me as though I'm a nuisance.

"Listen. I don't want to be a pest. Heck, it was gracious of you to bring me along, but leaving me locked in this car was not cool." I needed to get that off my chest.

Maggie drives, focusing on what's ahead. "Point noted."

"And my cell phone doesn't work."

"No, it doesn't."

It's evident that I'm really getting on her nerves. I've known Maggie long enough to be able to tell when she's tense, because she bites her lip. She's doing that now.

"So… what happened in there?" I ask.

"You're about to find out."

"Have you agreed to meet Stacy somewhere?"

Maggie looks at me as if I'm dense or something.

"What?" I ask.

The driver of the truck beeps his horn like a madman as the guy in the passenger seat hops out and trots over to the sidewalk. He's out of sight, but I presume he's halting sidewalk traffic. Maggie drives so close to the truck that it looks like the front of the vehicles are touching. Suddenly, what's happening here makes sense.

I point to the truck. "They're with you?"

Maggie nods once. That's her way of saying yes.

As a truck backs out, we pull out right behind it. The guy did a really good job of halting traffic on the sidewalk and the first lane of the street. And Maggie does a great job of capitalizing on his effort.

We drive behind the truck for a while, but then it veers off to the right and we keep straight.

"All right, Dais. You wanted your chance to bat. Well, you're up next."

I frown, confused. "Please elaborate."

She explains step-by-step where we're going and my role in what we're doing next.

"You can always sit in the car and wait. Once you see what you're going to see, you can never unsee it." She backs up her grave warning with a glance in my direction.

I consider Ed. Maggie is a mother as well, and what she does doesn't make Abel a psycho maniac. Granted, I have no idea what we're about to do.

"Do I have to kill someone?"

She chuckles. "No."

I'm glad she thought that was funny. Now I'm relieved that I don't have to hurt anyone.

"Are you going to kill someone?" I ask.

She just glares straight ahead. She pauses too long, and that just might be my answer.

"Are you?" I press.

"I don't want to."

"But if you have to?"

She's silent again. Finally, she glances at me as we turn onto the Brooklyn Bridge. "I've never had to kill anyone in my life, Daisy, but I can never say *never.*"

Every muscle in my body tenses up. *Dang it, Daisy. This is no joke.* I'm starting to seriously question why I insisted on tagging along. I guess I thought that she would pressure Stacy for answers and somehow do it without the use of force. Stacy would tell us exactly where to find my husband. After which I would have my one true love in my life again, Ed would have his father, Charlie would have his brother, and we'd all live happily ever after. What a fairy tale.

We've been turning down different streets in Brooklyn for the longest time, and it feels as if we're getting nowhere very quickly. Finally, we pull into the subterranean parking lot of a luxury high-rise apartment complex that doesn't look quite finished. As we descend into the depths of this gloomy structure layer by layer, it feels as though our being here is a dark secret.

Maggie parks in front of a door. She studies me as if she's searching to see if I am going to be up for what comes next. I straighten my posture and look confidently into her eyes.

"I'm ready," I say, making sure my tone is resolute.

She still hasn't taken her eyes off me. I'm wondering if she's having second thoughts.

"From this point on, you don't speak until I say you can. Got it?"

I nod spastically because I'm so nervous.

She leans over to open the glove compartment. "Put these on." She takes out a pair of black gloves, hands them to me, and then puts a pair over her own hands.

After she sees that mine are on, she turns toward her door. "Let's go." Maggie gets out of the car, and so do I.

Through the door, there's a set of elevators. Maggie presses the button. We get in, and she doesn't press another button, but we go up. I want to ask her who's operating the elevator right now but remember that I'm to remain quiet. The elevator stops on one of the floors. I have no idea which. I follow Maggie down a sterile hallway. I study the back side of her. Maggie is about an inch and a half taller than I am. She's always been slender but not bony. Her black pants hug her thighs and butt. She's still thin but also muscular, powerful. And the way she's walking, a mugger definitely wouldn't want to make the mistake of attacking her in a dark alley. I can tell she can beat the stew out of most men.

She turns to face a door, and before touching the handle, there's a click. The light on the panel next to the door flashes green. She opens the door and walks boldly in.

This is one big, empty room. Construction hasn't even begun yet. In the corner, next to the floor-to-ceiling windows, sits a big brown box. Maggie walks over, opens it, and takes out what looks like a cross between a beekeeper's suit and a space suit.

She hands me the bottoms and top of the costume and gives me a look that says, *Put this on*. It definitely will not be convenient to wear over my skirt suit, so I strip to my underwear and then put on the suit, which is made of vinyl. Maggie puts the suit on over the clothes she's wearing. Next, she takes black hoods out of the box. I'm pretty sure I'm supposed to put on one of those. There's some sort of screen material over where holes for the eyes and mouth are cut. It doesn't look as if it will be easy to breathe, speak, or see. But the deal was to not question her, and I do as I'm told. I put on the hood. Surprisingly, I can see and breathe perfectly fine. I feel Maggie's hands doing something with the back of my suit. There must be some sort of control panel in it.

"Are you comfortable?" I believe Maggie asked that question. However, her voice was distorted.

I guess I can speak now. "Um, yeah." My voice is distorted too.

She says, "Good. Here's what's going to happen…"

I listen attentively.

MY HEART IS KNOCKING HARD. I CAN FEEL THE vibration at the base of my throat. Maggie and I just left that apartment and entered another one, which was two doors down.

It's dim in here, and the black walls catch me off guard. Also, it looks as if there are no windows. As I peer at where the floor-to-ceiling windows should be, I can see that they've been covered with plywood and also painted black.

"Who's there?" a faint and trembling voice says.

Maggie has once again instructed me to not speak unless spoken to. I follow her around a wall, and we enter a room. There sits Stacy Pruitt, chained to a chair with her hands behind her back and a black cover over her eyes, which Maggie snatches off. I do as instructed and stand behind a metal table with instruments laid on top of it. The longer I study them, the more I see. There are syringes, knives, and some sort of pliers with the sharp edges. The first thought that comes to my mind is the F word. Like, really—fuck! What in the world is Maggie about to do?

"Who the fuck are you?" Stacy spits.

"Let's get something clear," Maggie says in her distorted voice. "You care about staying alive more than I care about you staying alive."

"Fuck you!" Stacy yells and then spits on Maggie's suit.

"What's your business with Laura Altman?"

Stacy just glares at her. I'm frozen stiff, wondering what Maggie is going to do to make her talk. I don't think Stacy understands that Maggie is willing to go all the way to get whatever she needs out of her.

"Three," Maggie says.

She's talking to me. I look down. The sharp pliers are directly aligned with a red-painted number three. I hold them up. Maggie waits a moment before she takes them from me. I think it's because she wants Stacy to get a clear picture of what she's about to use to torture her. Stacy is watching as if wondering how far this person is willing to go.

Maggie grabs her earlobe. Thank goodness neither of them can see how squeamish I am under this hood, especially when Maggie puts those pliers around Stacy's ears and begins to close them.

Stacy screams, "Help! Stop! Okay!"

It's too late—she's already bleeding. But at least Maggie didn't cut her ear all the way off. My head is spinning, stomach turning as I fight the urge to faint and vomit.

"She's blackmailing us!"

"Who do you mean by *us*?"

"I don't know who the fuck you are, but you know who the fuck I am, so just take a guess," Stacy says while breathing heavily.

"One," Maggie says.

I've been watching with bated breath, so it takes a

moment to realize she's talking to me. I pick up the syringe and wait for Maggie to take it from me.

Stacy's eyes grow wide. "I'm no good to you dead."

"But you're only good to me if you're telling the truth," Maggie says.

I'm pretty confused about what Maggie's about to do. She still has the pliers, which she moves to Stacy's other ear, and before Stacy can plead for her to not do it, Maggie clamps down.

Stacy screams. Maggie rushes over to take the syringe and injects her with whatever was in the tube. I think I just learned that I don't have the constitution for what's going on in this room. Gradually, Stacy begins to calm down. She's groggy and becoming more lethargic by the second. I want to ask Maggie if Stacy's dying and why she would kill her before she could tell us more about Belmont.

Stacy closes her eyes. Maggie takes off her hood. My mouth is caught open.

"Stacy Pruitt, what's your agent number?" Maggie asks in a soothing voice.

"324639," Stacy says.

Maggie pauses. "Good. Very good. You're telling me the truth. Are you ready to continue with no lies?"

"I'm ready to continue with no lies."

I'm amazed by what's happening.

"Why is Laura Altman blackmailing the agency?"

"It's not only Laura Altman. Certain board members of Lord & Lord Enterprises are blackmailing us."

"Why?"

"They discovered that Jack Lord is a security agent."

"Why didn't the agency deny their accusation?"

"They have proof of operation Black Eagle, which was completed by Red Cloud and without minimum impact."

Once again, Maggie is very still. It's as if she's listening to someone I can't hear. Finally, she nods.

"What did the board ask for?"

"That Jack Lord be expired."

Maggie quickly turns to the side. "Has he been expired?"

"Jack Lord has been off the grid since November 30 of last year."

"Let me try asking this way. Does the agency know where he is?"

"Yes."

"Is he alive?"

"Yes."

Maggie rubs her chin. "Is Belmont Jaxson Lord still Belmont Jaxson Lord?"

"No."

Maggie presses her hand over her heart. "Do you know what identity he has assumed?"

"No. It's classified."

"Who prepared his classification?"

Stacy frowns. Her eyes are still closed. "That's classified."

Maggie's shoulders slump.

"However, I have been searching for Jack Lord ever since he's gone missing."

"Why?" Maggie asked eagerly.

"I love him."

Volts of resentment shoot through my body as I remember those emails she sent me. I can't believe she hasn't gotten over my husband yet.

This time, Maggie turns all the way around and looks at me. Her eyes are sympathetic as she mouths, "Sorry."

I shake my head. It's okay. There's a lot to love about Belmont.

"And what has your search turned up?"

"Red Cloud was processed by agent 764932."

After a moment, Maggie looks at me and says, "Two."

I look down at the table at the second syringe. I hold it up. Maggie takes it and injects Stacy with whatever's in the tube. Stacy is immediately knocked out.

"You can take your hood off," Maggie says.

She walks over to the table to some kind of gun-shaped device. She takes it, goes to Stacy, raises her arm, and shoots her in the rib cage with it.

"I'm tagging her," she says. "The agency might find my bug, and they might not, but as long as she's wearing it, I can track her and know who she's talking to and what she's saying."

I still can't get over all the blood that's streaming out of the cuts in Stacy's ears.

"What are you going to do with her now?" I ask.

"Cleanup will handle her. We should get out of here."

I take one last look at Stacy as we walk out of the room. This entire incident feels like we're trapped in an episode of *The Twilight Zone* or something. We go back into the other room. I take off my suit and put my clothes on, and so does Maggie.

We're back in the car, and I can't believe how much my hands are still trembling. I catch Maggie glancing at them.

"How about I take you home?" she asks.

I nod stiffly. "Okay." I fight like hell to keep myself from crying. Gosh, that was so dramatic.

We don't say a word to each other until after she drives me back to the spot where we picked up this car. She stops behind Irwin, who's already in front of the building, waiting for me.

"I'll know where Jack is by morning. Meet me at my place by nine a.m."

"Okay." My voice is still shaky.

I turn to get out of the car, but Maggie takes me by the shoulder. "I knew you were determined to go with me. I'm sorry you had to see that, Daisy."

"It's okay. Thanks for not taking me to see more." I crack a tiny smile.

She smiles back. Her smile grows broader. "He's alive," she says, sounding as if she wants to cry about it.

"I heard."

"I'm going to find him."

I squeeze her hand. "I love you."

"Love you too."

The cold air mugs me as I step out of the car. It's nighttime. I can't believe how long all of that took. I make it into the safety of my apartment, and Ed is ecstatic that I'm home. He's screaming for me after hearing the elevator open. Once again, he's in the kitchen with Susan, eating. I kiss his face. I'm so happy for him that his dad is alive. However, I've been mulling something over. Stacy said that Belmont Jaxson Lord is no longer Belmont Jaxson Lord. What did she mean by that?

TONIGHT, ED SLEEPS WITH ME. I WANTED TO KEEP HIM close. I don't know why I have these weird, unidentifiable feelings. I want to cry. I want to rejoice. But most importantly, I feel that Belmont may be alive but whatever they've done to him will have transformed him forever.

CHAPTER FOURTEEN

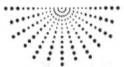

MAGGIE ADAMS

*G*rey was in my ear the entire time I was questioning Stacy. He ran whatever he could find on agent 764932, and we came up with Da Chung Chin, a foreign agent. So the out-of-country contacts questioned him. They were more brutal than I could be. Within two hours, Grey had securely hacked the agency's mainframe, having only thirty seconds to find what he could about Meyer Schulz in Homer, Alaska, before their security software would be able identify and locate the intruder.

Daisy sits very still and listens very patiently as I explain. She's a hard one to read. I'm still waiting for some sort of reaction that will give me an idea of how to proceed.

"Is Belmont going by the name Meyer Schulz?" she asks.

"Yes, he is."

"But from what you said and Stacy insinuated, he believes he is this person. Is that correct?"

Here's more that I've noticed about Daisy. She's very pragmatic. Sometimes she comes off as cold and unemotional. Before Monroe really got to know Daisy, she would refer to her as *the wet rag*. Daisy looks unaffected as she runs whatever information she's processing through all the channels in her brain. Basically, I'm playing chess with her. I don't want her to accompany me on this journey. It's dangerous and could be downright deadly.

"Yes," I say.

Daisy nods as if she's pondering something. "What's your plan, Maggie?"

"Truthfully, it will all depend on Jack's reaction. I can handle whatever comes next. However, it's best that I confront him alone."

"I agree that it's best. It was best for you to remain behind when Vince was abducted and Belmont had to find him. It was also best that I had nothing to do with what went on yesterday with Stacy Pruitt. There are lots of things that are best for me, Maggie, but I would like to be able to decide what those things are."

Fuck. I follow Daisy's eyes to my bag, which is sitting on the sofa.

"You can't call Susan to let her know that you may not be home tonight. Are you okay with that?" I keep my fingers crossed that the possibility of worrying Susan will make Daisy change her mind.

"I'm fine with it." She's unwavering.

I scrub my hand over my face, feeling the stress of it all. "We should get going, then."

"Yes, we should."

THE AGENCY HAS PUT A DETAIL ON ME, WHICH MEANS they're watching me. But I've figured out how to give them the slip. The security camera in the cargo elevator has been manipulated to feed them false real-time images. So as Daisy and I take that elevator to the rear of the building and exit into the alley, they still have no idea that I'm on the move. The alley is only about seven feet wide. Right across from the rear exit of my building is one to another building. It's always locked. Tenants are not allowed to go in or out, but I have a key that deactivates the alarm system when I turn it. As soon as we enter this neighboring structure, there's a door to the right that remains locked until I unlock it from the alley. We take the stairs down and move through another narrow hallway, which has cement floors and walls. Daisy hasn't made a peep while following me. She's definitely better at following instruction than I was when Jack took me on the mission to find Vince. I glance back at her just to make sure she's doing okay. She smiles slightly. She's fine.

At the end of the hallway, there's a door, a tight space, and then another door. We're moving through buildings. After the third one, we walk up another set of short stairs and take the elevator up to the roof, where a helicopter is waiting.

"That was pretty elaborate," Daisy says.

"I aim to please."

We chuckle, which makes this grave moment feel lighter.

The helicopter takes us to Pittsburgh, where we board a private flight to Chinitna Bay, Alaska. I'm still waiting for Daisy to ask more questions, but she doesn't. When the flight takes off and we're squarely in the air, she doesn't say a thing. Instead, she gazes out the window thoughtfully.

"Are you okay?" I ask.

She slowly turns to face me. "I don't know yet."

"Do you have any questions?"

"How?" Her eyes were watery.

"How what?"

"How could they possibly make my husband forget who he is?"

I'm hardwired to not disclose classified methods. But she's already ventured pretty far down the rabbit hole, so what's another ten miles?

"It's a method that causes consistent brain damage." I shift squeamishly in my seat. "At least, I think that's the method they used on him."

Her entire face collapses into a severe frown. "His brain is damaged?"

Now comes the hard part. Just thinking about it scares me to death.

"So here's what they do. A smart chip may have been inserted into Jack's brainstem. That chip is communicating with three other chips, which have been inserted into the frontal lobe, temporal lobe, and occipital lobe of Jack's cerebral cortex. Some real smart people have figured out a way to feed Jack's cerebral cortex with false memories. If at any point his brain veers off of their script, the main chip in the brainstem is programmed to stop Jack from breathing and his heart from beating."

"Killing him?" Daisy says in her pragmatic way.

"Yes."

We stare at each other. Her expression is grave.

"How do you plan to keep my husband alive?"

"I'm going to kick his ass."

She studies me, I think to make sure I'm joking, but I'm not. I've been trained to give Jack the fight of his life.

Finally, Daisy erupts into laughter. "Are you kidding me?"

I shake my head and look as serious as I can. "Not in the least. In order to turn Jack off, I have to put him into a deep nonconscious state."

"How do you plan to do that?"

"I told you. I have to fight him, and I have to win."

She quickly turns her whole body to face me. "No," she says, shoving her finger at me.

I sit up straight. She says it with such authority that I have to take a moment to remember who's in charge here.

"Have someone else do it, Maggie," she says.

"There is no one else. The network of people that I can trust at the moment is very small, and out of all of them, I may have the most success because he taught me everything he knows about combat."

Daisy sighs and closes her eyes. "What about me?"

"What about you? You can't fight Jack. He will kill you at first sight. This Meyer Schulz character doesn't know you, Daisy." I say it strongly because I want to make it clear that this man is not her husband, and he's not my cousin. Meyer Schultz is a trained assassin ready to kill anyone who confronts him.

Her forehead wrinkles and straightens and then wrinkles again. After scratching the back of her head, Daisy faces forward. "One step at a time."

I study her suspiciously. I'm not quite sure what she means by that, or I'm very sure what she means by that. I don't want to rock the boat. But I'm definitely ready to make sure she doesn't get herself killed.

"Anyway, how's Abel?" Daisy asks.

I want to ask if she's purposely changing the subject. However, there's no need to ask. She clearly is doing just that. And I'll play along. We have a six-hour flight ahead of us. It's best that we stay civil.

"He's fine." I settle into my seat.

She closes her eyes. "Good. That's because you and Vince have done an amazing job giving him a home and love, the two most important things a human being can have."

"Thanks, Dais. We've been trying really hard to make his life stable. Things could've gone one way or another, you know. Lucky for us, they've gone the right way."

She grunts warmly and smiles. "I love the sound of that."

"So what do you think about the board of directors being tied to this whole ordeal?" I ask.

Daisy turns to look at me. "Truthfully?"

"It's the only way I want it."

"I have no idea, but I want fucking heads to roll." That look in her eyes is pure anger and hate.

I feel it too. "Maybe I can help you with that."

"Promise?"

"Promise."

The rest of the flight is quiet. We've tried small talk and found that now is not the time for it. No. We must sit and stew in our bitter fear and anger along with the antithesis of those emotions, which is hope.

ABOUT THREE HOURS INTO THE FLIGHT, DAISY AND I

force down turkey club sandwiches and spring-greens salad. Afterward, I go into the secured control room to make sure we still have eyes on Meyer Schulz. I didn't tell this to Daisy, but this morning, he just returned from an assignment in Croatia. He knew nothing about the man he was supposed to expire. And he probably felt nothing when he did it. The agency had many options when it came to taking care of the board of directors' threat. What they decided—to snatch Jack away from the ones he loves—should've been their last resort, not their first.

Last night, as Vince and I lay loose-limbed in bed, we discussed all the ways I could exact revenge on the agency. I was surprised he didn't stop me and talk some sense into me. Perhaps he knew that I was angry and was just allowing me to express it. I'm sure he knew I would never do anything to jeopardize his or Abel's safety. And with all of that said, I still want to bring the agency to its knees. After Grey and I confirm that my imminent interaction with Jack is a go, I return to the cabin, take my seat, close my eyes, and contemplate new ways to attack and destroy the agency.

CHAPTER FIFTEEN

MEYER SCHULZ (BELMONT LORD)

*H*e knew to clean his boots before he entered the cabin. His boots always transferred remnants of the time spent away back to the cabin. He didn't want to track any of it inside. No reminders. Not one.

There wasn't much in the small space—one sofa, a chair, a rug in front of the fireplace with its constantly roaring fire, the dining room table in front of a small kitchen, and the cot he slept on. He supposed his life was bleak, but he wasn't quite sure. He sat patiently day in and day out, waiting.

It was getting close to dinnertime. He had to eat in order to keep up his strength. The sun had descended, but when it rose again, he would dress himself in the blue suit and his newly cleaned pair of black boots and be transported to his next assignment.

That night's meal would be five and a half ounces of top sirloin steak, seven large eggs combined with five cups of low-fat milk and protein powder, seven and a half ounces of grilled tilapia, and two cups of steamed broccoli. He had supplements as well, some to take in the morning and some to ingest at night. It took forty-five minutes to prepare the meal. It took fifteen minutes for him to sit and consume every morsel.

After dinner, he stripped out of his trousers and sweater and put on his jogging pants and sweatshirt. He was going for a nighttime run. That was the only time of the day he was allowed out of his house, other than when he was leaving for an assignment.

Meyer sat on the sofa in the same spot he normally sat in, tying his right athletic shoe. And then he heard it—a twig crunching beneath a foot, which stepped ever so gently. He let go of his shoestring and sat up straight. And then he stood. He closed his eyes as his arm slowly moved away from his body. His limb could feel the invading energy. It was close. He looked up at the wooden ceiling. A slight creaking came from the right, and he shot his face in that direction. *Stay on the offense, but never walk into a trap.* He moved carefully across the room. His back hugged the wall. There were only three ways in, and he had a bird's-eye view to each point of access.

There was a loud bang. Abruptly, the door blew open, and Meyer jumped off the wall and faced the trespasser.

"Ugh." He felt a sharp pain in the middle of his back as he fell forward. He had been kicked. He had been tricked. He was no longer on the offensive. Next came a blow to the head. It hurt like hell and made his eyesight foggy. But he could see her after that, a slight but powerful woman with brown hair, pale skin, and the face of an angel. Too bad he would have to send the celestial being to hell.

Meyer spun and got low enough to trip her. He knocked her off her feet, but she was able to recover in an instant. Who was this woman? He came back with a direct hit to her kidney. She absorbed his strike and elbowed him in the groin. Oh, the fucking agony. He often fought through pain, though. He spun and knocked her in the back, and she hit the floor. He jumped on top of her and clenched her neck.

"Belmont?" a woman shouted.

He turned to the doorway. The face. The woman. *Her face.* Something sharp pierced him in the neck, and the next thing he knew, there was nothing.

CHAPTER SIXTEEN

"*E*xtraction team, get in here stat," Maggie yells and then turns her fiery glare on me. "I told you to stay put!"

I part my lips to speak. I want to defend myself. Didn't I just save her hide? However, after watching her struggle with Belmont, I can see that her warning for me to stay put was real.

Maggie and I arrived at the land surrounding this remote cabin about half an hour ago. When our flight from Pittsburgh first landed on the airstrip in Chinitna Bay, Maggie gave me a heavy coat, boots, stocking cap, and gloves. She put on the same garb, and then we disembarked into the chilly night. A helicopter was waiting for us not too far away. I followed Maggie as she trotted through the high grass toward our ride. We boarded. My body trembled as we soared over the ocean. Maggie kept her eyes pointed straight ahead. I figured there was no need to discuss where we were going and what was going to happen. It was all happening. There was no turning back.

The helicopter dropped us off in the deep, dark, unlit woods. After walking through brush for a while with only a flashlight to illuminate our path, we ran into a muddy road where two unshaven men wearing camouflage jackets over plaid shirts were leaning against a dark-colored jeep. At first, I thought they were hunters and we were just crossing paths. But Maggie quickly identified them as the extraction team. We climbed into the backseat and went for a ride that lasted about half an hour.

We finally stopped. "Stay put," Maggie whispered with a severe look of warning in her eyes.

"Of course I will." I was lying. "But I do want to get out and stretch my legs."

Maggie hesitated. She studied me as if she was trying to ascertain whether or not I could be trusted. For as long as I've known her, I never gave her a reason to not trust me until then.

She hopped out of the backseat, and I scooted out

behind her. And without another word, she traipsed off into the deep, dark woods.

I had an insane and intense drive to see my husband as this man who forgot his own name. The two men dressed as hunters kept a good eye on me. It was too dark to get a good look at their faces, but I guessed they were in their midthirties. Then one of them cursed under his breath and mumbled something about forgetting to set a map. The other whispered something about how that would've been a huge fuckup. And while they were distracted by what could've been, I swiftly and quietly dashed into the woods. I tried to stay as close as possible to the spot Maggie had entered. I'd been a travel writer so many years that exploring foreign territory came easily. If there was no trail, then I would create my own. Follow one straight line, and if it led to nowhere, then take it back to where it first began. Call it luck or fate, but when I ran into a weather-beaten wooden fence, I knew I was near my husband's cabin. I veered to the right, leaving my perfectly drawn trail behind. After walking along the fence for a while, I saw a trail and took it, and it led me to a rustic cabin.

From where I stood, I could hear banging and things crashing. Maggie had said she would have to fight him, and that was exactly what I heard—a tussle. I ran as fast as I could to the front door. I didn't want Belmont to hurt her or vice versa. Without a thought, I flung the door open. When I saw him choking Maggie, I had to scream his name to stop him from making the one mistake he would never forgive himself for.

Our gazes locked. Then Maggie stabbed him in the neck with a needle.

"Shit. He saw you and reacted," Maggie says.

I shake my head. I'd forgotten why that was so detrimental until now. Maggie already explained how the chips in his brain are connected. If he recognized me, then he could stop breathing.

Maggie's on her knees beside him with two fingers pressed against the soft, hollow area on the side of his neck. "Fuck!"

I'm frantic. "Does he have a pulse?"

"Jack. Come on, Jack." She's performing chest compressions and rescue breathing on him.

I'm shaking, and the room is spinning, but I don't want to pass out. If his heart has stopped and he's no longer breathing, there's no way he's going to survive long enough to receive medical attention.

The two men race through the front entrance, carrying orange containers that look like coolers. I

ADORE HER, MORE OF HER

expected them to have a stretcher to put him on and race him back to the jeep. Maggie stands up and moves out of the way so they can take over. They stick probes into Belmont's skin. Blood trickles from the points of entry.

"Ready," one says.

"Activate the map," the other says.

Belmont's body jumps. His eyes open wide, and he convulses. I press my hand over my heart. Tears roll from my eyes. I hardly recognize Belmont. He has a beard, and he's very buff. His windblown hair is cut very short and dyed blond. I want to pinch myself and wake up from this nightmare. I want it to be November 30 of last year. I want to be standing in the window, waiting for him to come home. I want to see the headlights of his SUV turn onto our long driveway, heading toward the house. I want my heart to dance, happy that he's here where I'll be able to kiss him, hug him, and tell him how much I love him. He would tell me how his day went. I would love hearing about all the drama associated with his business, and he would equally and attentively listen to me in the same way. He would play with Ed for a while, and I would let them have their time together. Then he'd put our child to sleep and go to bed, where he would hold me so close our hearts would feel as though they had become one.

Suddenly, Belmont's body stops quaking, and his eyes close.

"Contained," one of the guys says.

The other stands. "Let's move him out." He runs outside and comes back with a stretcher. The two men load Belmont on it.

"Time to go." Maggie waits for me to follow them out.

I'm still pretty disappointed in myself for not following her directions. The jeep is parked right in front of the door. They put Belmont in the back. I want to lie with him, but I know I can't. Once we're all in, the vehicle takes off, driving quickly through the brush, barely missing trees, and bouncing as the wheels roll over whatever is on the ground.

Maggie and I happen to look at each other at the same time.

"Sorry," I say.

"It's okay. But I want you to know that it wasn't as bad as it looked. I had him where I wanted him."

"Choking you?"

"Preoccupied with choking me so that I could inject him with the serum."

"Again, I'm so sorry."

She takes my hand. "Stop apologizing. I would've done the same thing. Now it's over. It's time to see which version of Jack we're left with."

UNFORTUNATELY, WE ARE FORCED TO PART WAYS AT the airport. Maggie goes with Belmont on one airplane, and I take another flight home. I've already crossed the thick line by not staying put like I should've, which almost cost my husband his life, so this time, I figure I won't make a stink about separating from him. He's in the right hands now, and that's all that matters.

It's 7:34 a.m. when I walk into the apartment. Traces of light from the kitchen flow into the living room.

"Daisy?" Susan calls.

"It's me."

"She's here." She sounds relieved.

"Where have you been?" Fred sternly says before we see each other.

Suddenly, my cell phone rings in my briefcase. I reach my hand inside it, eagerly looking for the phone. I find it. The screen tells me it's Maggie.

Susan and Fred walk into the room, and they

look as if they experienced many hours of worry. I raise a finger to let them know I will address their fears as soon as possible.

"Hello, Maggie," I say.

"Turn on the news. Try BCN." She hangs up.

"Are you going to tell us where you were?" Susan says, shaking her hands.

"We found Belmont." Heck—I may as well tell her. I'm pretty sure the agency already discovered that little tidbit of information.

Susan gasps, and Fred looks as if he's been hit by a Mack truck.

"Where?" she exclaims.

"Just follow me," I say impatiently. I have a feeling we're about to learn more.

Once we're in the living room, I find the remote control and turn on the TV. I don't have to change the channel. There's a special report playing on the TV already.

"Missing billionaire Jack Lord has been found alive…"

Belmont is sitting amongst a swarm of cameras with Maggie right next to him. He's wearing a dark-brown sweater, and I've never seen him look so exhausted. Maggie's in an impeccable gray suit jacket with a royal-blue silk blouse. She has an air of resilience and sophistication about her.

"Where have you been, Mr. Lord?" a reporter shouts.

"He cannot answer at the moment," Maggie says.

"Who found him?" another reporter asks.

"He wishes to remain unnamed for now," Maggie says.

The questions are flying, and Belmont still looks flummoxed.

"Mr. Lord, will you resume your position as CEO of Lord & Lord Enterprises?"

"Mr. Lord, have you heard of the purging of senior executives and board members at Lord & Lord Enterprises?"

I steal a glance at Fred, who nods, letting me know I've heard correctly.

"I can confirm that Mr. Lord's disappearance is directly related to the purge," Maggie says.

A rumble of shocked exclamations erupts.

"My God, he looks so different," Susan says.

Fred looks at me with a deep scowl. "What Maggie just said—is that true?"

"Yes." Just saying that word makes my tight throat ache.

"Where *did* you find him?" Fred asks.

I fold my arms. For some reason, just thinking about the conditions he lived in brings tears to my eyes. "In a remote cabin in Alaska."

"Are you insinuating that foul play was involved?" a reporter on TV asks.

"I'm not insinuating. An official investigation is underway. And those who are responsible for Mr. Lord's disappearance will be brought to justice. In time, Mr. Lord will be resuming his role as captain of Lord & Lord Enterprises, but his colleague Jetson Gordon will serve as CEO until the transition has been completed."

"What about Mrs. Lord?" someone asks.

Belmont abruptly sits up straight and glares in the direction of whoever asked that question.

"It's pretty obvious that she wants to remain close to her husband. What his family has suffered is devastating. And they ask that you respect their privacy."

"Aren't you related?"

"You already know the answer to that question, Andrew." Maggie quickly stands and waves her hand. "Thank you all for coming."

Belmont stands as well. He looks like a ticking time bomb that's very close to exploding.

Reporters continue asking questions as they

walk off the scene, and I turn off the television before I have to listen to talking heads analyze what we've just seen. One of them has already started talking about how despondent Mr. Lord appears.

Susan looks at me with a wide-eyed expression, shaking her head. "What in the world is going on?"

"It's too much to explain," I say.

Fred's cell phone buzzes. He takes it out of his pocket, reads the screen, and then writes a text message. The phone immediately dings again. He writes something else.

"That's Maggie. I have to go."

"Where?" I say.

He shakes his head as he hightails it to the elevator. "Can't say, but I'm sure Maggie will be in touch."

I feel lost as he gets into the elevator and the doors close. However, I also feel relieved that it looks as though I have more time to prepare before my biggest fear walks through that door.

I fold my fingers against my chest, squeezing my hands together as I contemplate what's best for Ed. I'm not even sure Belmont's coming home to be with me. He looked so confused. Perhaps he's not stable and will need to spend more time under medical supervision. Regardless, I want to be here for him.

There's no better time than the present to take my mom up on her offer.

"What can I get you?" Susan says.

I didn't notice her standing behind me.

"Could you get Ed packed?"

Thinking about having to send our son away for a while feels like a dagger in my heart. I love his scent in the air and his gentle energy that constantly fills the house.

"Where's he going?" Susan asks.

"It would be nice if one look at Ed would make Belmont remember every bit of our happy life together. But I can't put fantasyland before our son's safety. He's going to stay with my mom. Would you be able to accompany him on the flight?"

Susan shows me a wavering smile. "Of course." Her tone is lackluster.

I sigh before delivering the second bit of bad news. "You're going to have to leave as well. I'm just not sure how safe it is for anyone to be around Belmont. At least, not for a while." I let my pleading gaze caress her face. I have a feeling she's fallen in love with this city. I'm also asking her to put physical distance between her and Fred.

Susan folds her arms and quickly turns to gaze off into the distance. "How soon?"

"I'm calling my mom now."

She nods but walks over to give me a big, tight hug. "I'm happy for you. I'm not sure what's going on with Jack, but at least he's alive."

"Thanks for all you've done. I mean it—thanks."

One last squeeze, and when we let go, she heads down the hallway to pack for Ed.

I call my mom just as she's about to call me. She tells me she saw the press conference, and I say I don't have much time to talk. When I ask if she's still willing to keep Ed for a while, she enthusiastically says yes and agrees that I should take Ed out of the house as fast as I can if I feel Belmont might be dangerous. I believe a large part of her is looking out for Ed's safety, but there's also a small part that just wants him all to herself.

When the call ends, I contact my aircraft services and schedule Susan and Ed's flight. The phone rings as I walk to Ed's room, wanting to spend as much time with him as I can. It's Charlie. He saw the press conference and says that he's on his way to New York.

Ed is standing in his crib. He looks too big for the bed. I've been too busy to shop for a new one. I pick him up, and he clings to me. I take him to my room to change his diaper and tell him he'll stay with grandma Heloise for a while. I also tell him that Daddy is alive and he'll see Daddy as soon as he's well. Ed must've understood much of what I said, because he's extra clingy this morning. I dress him in warm corduroy pants and a thick sweater because the airplane is often very cold. Then I take him into the kitchen and sit him in his high chair, and we sing the ABC song and some Barney songs as I cook one scrambled egg and a bowl of sliced bananas and strawberries.

Thirty minutes later, it's time for him to go. I hold him in my arms as Susan and I walk to the elevator.

"Mommy's going to see you soon," I say.

The corners of his mouth turn down, and he sniffs before making the transition into full-fledged crying.

"You're going to be okay," I say, bouncing him.

"Let me have him," Susan says.

Ed clings so tightly to my shirt that he wouldn't fall even if I let go of him, which I'd never do.

Suddenly, the elevator opens. My mouth is caught open in awe. Ed instantly stops bawling.

"I saw you," Belmont says. Maggie is beside him.

"Yes," I'm only barely able to say.

Ed rests his head on my shoulder as he stares at Belmont.

Belmont opens and closes his mouth and then studies Ed for a long moment. "Ed?"

"Yes," Maggie and I say at the same time.

Maggie smiles. "You remember him?"

Belmont's frown deepens. "Yes." As he closes his eyes and stands in his sadness, I so badly want to hug him. But there's an energy he's emitting, one that begs for distance.

I clear my throat and gulp nervously. "Ed's going to stay with my mom for a while."

"No," Belmont emphatically says.

Susan and I look at each other. Her eyebrows are squished together, and I can feel that mine are too.

She shrugs, and I shrug back.

CHAPTER SEVENTEEN

*B*elmont is emotionally distant. I'm sure he remembers me, but I'm not sure in what way. I showed him our wedding photos, vacation photos, family pictures, and photos that were taken after we brought Ed home from the hospital. He seems to have no visceral reaction to any of the images. However, he lethargically says that he remembers them. Something is definitely wrong with him.

Before Maggie leaves, she asks if he wants to lie down for a while. His gaze bounces to Ed, and he says, "Yes."

"I'll show you to the room," I say.

"That's not necessary. I remember."

"Oh, okay." The fact that he doesn't want my

company stings a little. The old Belmont would've said yes just so he could be near me. I've also noticed that he doesn't sound the same.

Maggie and I watch as he walks down the hallway and turns the corner. She reaches over to massage my shoulder, making sure she has my complete attention. "He'll be fine. You'll be fine."

She hasn't blinked. I think she's communicating beyond the words she's using.

"Right." And then I remember something. "You know, Charlie's on his way."

Her lips press together in a slight grimace. "I did not know."

I've learned that when Maggie is in fixer mode, she sounds very formal.

"Do you think Belmont's up for company?"

She shakes her head but says, "Absolutely, yes."

I cross my arms, feeling extremely vulnerable. Apparently, our apartment is still bugged. I have tons of questions for Maggie right now. Is Belmont's brain normal? Is the agency going to come after him? Are they coming after her? Are we all sitting ducks? Knowing Maggie, there's a plan, and I would love to know what it is.

"You both get rest, and we'll talk in the morning," she says.

I nod. "Okay."

Maggie and I squeeze hands. She gives me one last probing look and then turns and walks into the elevator. I don't take my eyes off her until the doors close.

I stand there, feeling alone. Susan made the flight I scheduled, only instead of flying into Santa Monica, she flew to Santa Barbara and then home to Montecito. It's safer for her to be as far away from here as possible. Ed is still napping. I'm lost, not knowing what to do next. I haven't had downtime like this in so long.

I head to the living room. Each step I take feels like I'm either walking on air or being dragged down by gravity. Gosh, this living room is big. I'm surprised Belmont was able to survive in that cabin. He hates small spaces. I walk to the window. Talk about not being able to stop and smell the roses. I'm just noticing the foliage in the park is displaying fall colors—orange, yellow, red—nature's luxurious scene.

I haven't showered since my return. I didn't sleep very well on the airplane, either. The silence is relaxing. I retrieve the remote control, take off my house slippers, and sit on the sofa. I turn on the television and click away from the news channel until I land on the first movie. The dialogue, music, and sound effects just seem so loud. The tranquil feeling I was beginning to have before turning the TV on leaves my body.

I turn it off and rest my head on the backrest. I can't seem to get Alaska out of my mind. I see myself walking through that forest. It was still chilly. I wasn't afraid—I was eager. And then there was the first look between Belmont and me. He was choking Maggie. Could he end up choking me too? But the chips were removed from his brain. Is he damaged beyond repair? I'm picturing the many versions of him, starting from the moment he approached my table when we first met on Martha's Vineyard. He was charming. My heart was too broken to notice his electric hazel eyes, sexy, chiseled jawline, and pillowy lips that showcased his sexy smirk. Then we made love, and it was nothing like I've ever experienced. My heart was in it. My soul cried for him. His touch filled me with the kind of desire that makes one abandon reason. And goodness gracious, did I abandon reason. My eyes close, remembering every touch, deep kiss, and thrust of the first time we ever made love.

. . .

WHEN I OPEN MY EYES, NIGHT HAS FALLEN BEYOND the glass. I check the clock on the mantel. It's 8:38 p.m.

I gasp. "Ed."

I leap to my feet and race to his bedroom. I'm not surprised that he's not crying. Belmont and I are lucky in the way that Ed doesn't cry long. He'll eventually give up and find other ways to amuse himself.

When I make it to the doorway, I see Belmont standing in front of the window. He's holding Ed as they watch the city lights.

"Um, hi," I say carefully.

Belmont faces me. "He was crying, and you were asleep."

I part my lips to speak, but I'm lost for words, although my heart is filled with emotions. Ed is resting his face on his usual spot on Belmont's chest. How could I have ever thought he'd be in danger of his own father?

My lips form a slow smile. "I think he missed you very much." I flip the light on.

"Could you keep it off, please?" Belmont asks and then turns to face the city again. "We're just going to watch a little longer."

What in the world do I do now? I don't know how long he's been alone with Ed. If everything were peachy keen, I would go take a shower and let Belmont watch Ed. What's funny is that this is the way Belmont used to spend time with him before he went missing. But I'm still not convinced that Belmont won't snap at any moment. So I sit in the chair very quietly and wait until they're done watching the city.

About fifteen minutes later, Ed tells his dad and me that he's hungry.

"I can take him," I say.

Belmont sniffs the top of Ed's head. He closes his eyes to indulge. "I remember the smell."

I'm trapped in his gaze as he walks toward me.

He stops in front of me, puts his nose next to my ear, and sniffs deeply. Our gazes are stuck as he pulls back.

"I'm tired," he finally says and hands over Ed, who moans a little before the exchange is made.

Belmont walks away. How strange is that? I have to stand still to get my bearings before making Ed something to eat.

I prepare diced organic chicken with rice along with steamed carrots and a glass of milk. For me and Belmont, I warm leftovers from the dinner Susan prepared last night while I was away. It's so weird having Belmont in the house. I try to make the night feel as normal as I can for Ed. But he understands things are different, which is why I've stopped pretending. Neither of us have the wherewithal to study letters and numbers and dance to videos. We'd even started playing with children's learning programs on the computer in my office before going to bed, but we don't have the capacity for that, either. We sit on the sofa and watch the first Muppet movie ever made. Ed falls asleep before the second act is over. I take him to bed and then head to ours. My heart beats like a bass drum. Is it too soon to share the same bed? I take one deep breath before walking into the room. He's not in here. There's a guest room next door. I creep down the hallway and peek inside. He's lying on the bed.

When I make it back to our bedroom, I notice that he didn't sleep in our bed earlier, either. He's choosing to put distance between us. I don't know how I feel about that. However, I do know that I'm too exhausted to let it cause me any level of insomnia. So I shower, exfoliate, floss, lower the shades over the window, get into bed, get cozy with the duvet, and go directly to sleep.

I awaken with a start. Susan isn't here.

"Ed!" I dash out of bed. As soon as my feet hit the hallway, a scent tickles my nose. I slow down and peek into Ed's room. He's not there. I follow the sound of pots, water running, and children's sing-along music. When I make it to the kitchen, I see Ed sitting in his high chair with scrambled eggs and oatmeal around his mouth.

Belmont stands in front of the sink, drying his hands with a towel. "I made us breakfast."

I follow his eyes to the dining table. Scrambled eggs, strips of bacon, sliced fruit, and biscuits are set in the middle along with orange and coffee.

"You made all that?" I ask, pointing to the spread.

"Is it too much? I found biscuits in the refrigerator. I remember they're the ones you like."

They were the big country buttermilk biscuits from Santee Farms.

"You remembered?" I say.

Here he comes. I gulp nervously as we stand so close his personal energy washes over me. "There's a lot I'm remembering."

Belmont gently runs his finger from my shoulder down my arm. I skip a breath. It feels good to be touched by him again. Now he's gripping me by the small of my back. I stand, immobilized by the unknown. Here comes his face. Our lips touch. Our tongues do the same. My head floats above my shoulders. I'm weeping as we kiss and hold each other, knowing that I never want to let go.

I touch my lips and wait for my head to come back down to earth. "You kissed me."

He shrugs his eyebrows as if he's surprised by his own actions. "I did."

Belmont takes my hand and walks me to the table. He pulls out my chair, and I sit. This is definitely the husband I remember. As soon as we start eating, he tells me that we are now able to speak freely.

"Then they're not listening in anymore—the agency?" I say.

"No, they're not. First and foremost, I want to say that I love you. If I had known that I was separated from you and Ed, then I would've missed you a hell of a lot."

"I know, Belmont."

His jaw flexes like it normally does when he grinds his back teeth. He's angry.

"I have to go away a little while longer."

I blink as if I have to wake up from the dream in which he spoke the words I never wanted to hear. My gaze shifts to Ed, who's drinking from his bottle and pushing a button on his video-and-music machine.

"But why?" I am so sad.

"They won't stop until I shut them down."

"The agency?"

He frowns as if my mentioning them so casually disturbs him. "Yes. Right. And you're going to have to stay in this house until I'm back."

"Okay," I say, realizing it's the easiest thing he can ask me to do.

"A domestic will do the cooking, cleaning, and shopping and run any errands you'll need."

"I can cook my own meals, order my own groceries, and—"

He shakes his head adamantly. "I have to control who brings what into the apartment. Plus, Dallas is a great chef." He smiles.

I thought I'd never see him do that again. I search over my shoulder. "Is Dallas here now? Did he make all of this?"

Belmont chuckles. "I said I made breakfast, and I did."

"But you never make breakfast."

"I do now. It's the least I can do to make up for all you've done."

I imagine he's referring to running his company.

I frown earnestly because what I'm feeling comes from the bottom of my heart. "I'll do anything for you."

He clears his throat. "And I'll do anything for you."

We stare into each other's eyes as Ed plays a different song and starts singing along as best he can.

Belmont chuckles gently. I can't take my eyes off him. I can hardly believe we exist in this moment together, the three of us.

"So how's your brain?" I blurt. I'm curious about whether a flashback or PTSD will throw poison on the happy situation we have here.

"I got the rest I needed to help the swelling resolve." He points his smile at Ed, who grins and sings louder. "I missed a lot."

Should I reach out to take his hand? I'm still so very careful with him, but I don't know why. He's spoken the truth about missing a lot. And now he's going to leave again. I don't want to hint that I'm hurt about that, but I am, even if it's just slightly.

I gnaw nervously on my bottom lip.

"What is it?" Belmont asks.

"Huh?"

"You're chewing on your lip. What are you thinking?"

I want to tell him the truth, but it's so difficult to trust that I won't lose him again. Tears gloss over my eyes. All I can do is shrug. But I quickly remember Dr. Calvet insisting that I express my feelings to Belmont in a way that's clear and unambiguous.

I look down at my plate. "I'm just scared I'm going to lose you again—that's all."

I lift my gaze as Belmont gets up and sits beside me. He delicately strokes the side of my face. I'm staring into his glassy eyes. "You never lost me." He takes his hand away and returns to his seat. "Maggie told me how great a job you did running Lord & Lord Enterprises, and so did Fred."

I clear my throat. "Thanks."

"I knew if anything ever happened to me, you would be the one to take my place. I don't plan on ever leaving you for that long again. I know it's strange between us. We've got a lot of reacquainting to do." He has a naughty look in his eyes.

Ed slaps the table and says he wants to get out. I jump to my feet, but Belmont springs into action. "Let me."

"Sure," I say.

"I missed too much time with him."

He takes Ed to the sink and cleans his face with a wet paper towel. "By the way, are Fred and Susan a couple?"

I spread jelly over half a biscuit. "They went on a date a few days ago—well, not really a date. He came here for dinner. But I don't know if they're in a romantic relationship or not."

"He asked her to come back to the city, and she's staying with him." He turns the water off.

"Get out of here." I love this conversation we're having. It feels like old times.

"I've never seen him with a woman."

I tilt my head and look at him. "Have you seen him with a man?"

Belmont laughs, and it's contagious, because Ed laughs too. Then I laugh because they're laughing. And I let my heart relish this moment, one I thought I would never experience again, yet here I am, and here he is, and here we all are together.

After breakfast, Belmont kisses me good-bye at the elevator. There's just no easy way to do this. He has to go. I have to trust that he'll return. There's no use putting our son through another good-bye. Susan has taught Ed very well. He's playing with all of his toy instruments in his playroom. The music he's making doesn't sound bad at all. Some of the notes are connecting lyrically. He's definitely Jacques Blanchard's grandson.

Belmont inclines his ear in the direction of the music. "That's not so bad."

I fold my arms timidly. "Yeah, this is the first time I've heard him play like that. I've been working so much. Remember our schedule?"

He takes me in his arms. "We'll get back to normal. I promise you." His lips meet mine, our arms wrap around each other, and we kiss tenderly. My heart pulsates. I want him to hold me all day long and throughout the night. But he can't.

"I never stopped believing in you," I whisper as we stop kissing. "I won't stop now."

Belmont presses his lips against my forehead and then kisses it. My heart swells. He tells me security will be posted as soon as he's downstairs. They will be with us twenty-four, seven. The domestic team, which includes the great chef Dallas, will arrive in about an hour. They have their instructions. They'll be lodging in an apartment on the fourteenth floor.

I chuckle.

"What is it?" he asks.

"You truly are the same. You're always with the chefs."

"Hey, I cooked breakfast this morning. I can

hardly remember who I was while I was away, but I do remember doing a lot of cooking for myself."

I furrow my brow. I didn't know he doesn't remember being Meyer Schulz. He takes his thumb to smooth the pucker of skin between my eyes.

"Don't worry, baby."

I just smile. "I won't stop until you get home."

"Then I'll make it quick."

After one long, deep, warm kiss, he leaves. Just as he promised, two men ride up in the elevator and remain posted by the doors.

It's great to be home again. I catch up on laundry before the domestic team arrives. I love washing Ed's little clothes. I always sniff them before I put them into the wash and then take another whiff after clearing the dry cycle.

The domestic team arrives before I can clean out the refrigerator. Dallas, the famous chef, arrives with them. I insist on making Ed's lunch, but Dallas insists that I let him handle the cooking one time, and if I prefer to make my child's meals after that, he'll leave it in my hands. Of course, he whips ups the tastiest peach puree on little bits of whole-grain squares, green-bits salad, and homemade fish sticks.

I shake his hand. "You win." That's especially true

when I eat the same lunch as Ed and am totally satisfied.

Days merge into nights and stack up on top of each other. A week passes. I'm getting antsy, and this morning, I wake up and find a note at the foot of my bed. Belmont's name is written on the folded page, and the handwriting is his. Is he back?

I quickly unfold the paper.

I watched you sleep. You're so beautiful and soft. I can't lie next to you yet. My mission is half-complete.

I can't stop grinning as I press his letter against my heart.

CHAPTER EIGHTEEN

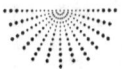

BELMONT LORD

*W*hen his feelings for Daisy returned, they came back with a vengeance. It should've been a sin to leave the warmth of her body and sweet kiss. The night before he headed out to set things right with the agency, he wanted very badly to sleep next to her. However, the medical specialists advised against it. This Meyer character that he once was could've come back and only stayed for a second, but that was all it would've taken for him to harm Daisy while she slept. He couldn't risk it.

The first week away from Daisy, he underwent more physical examinations and treatments. He needed to make sure he was one hundred percent healthy and his body clear of any tracking devices. He also worked with Grey to track Harold Doe.

The afternoon he was intercepted by Natasha in the parking garage, she'd told him that if he didn't go with her, then Daisy and Ed would be killed within seconds. He asked what her threat was about. She refused to offer answers and instead said he would find out when they arrived at their destination. Belmont drove until they reached the Oregon border, and then they switched seats. That was when she gave him the green pill, which was a drug to knock him out, and insisted that he take it. Belmont had a lot of familiarity with the green pill. He knew that if he held it in his mouth and consumed it slowly, he would feel groggy but be able to hear everything that was going on around him. So he pretended to swallow it by hiding it in the crease between his right chin and back teeth. When he opened his mouth to show Natasha, he had effectively hidden the tablet.

They had taken a long car drive, and their journey included a flight from Oregon to New Jersey. At one point, he could've taken out the pilots and escaped, but he had to figure out what the hell was going on. His family had been threatened, and that was an unforgivable offense.

They put him in a hospital room and checked his vitals. He knew the drill. A side effect of the green pill was an accelerated heartbeat and shortness of breath. He had neither. Belmont was then taken to an interrogation room, where they chained his wrists to a chair and feet to the ground. Webber Knight, agent 764932, was his intake agent.

"Why the fuck am I here like this?" he said, trying to raise his arm.

Knight casually wrote on the form attached to his clipboard. "Your shield has been compromised. You've been tasked for a level-eight reassignment," he said as if taking him away from his family was no sweat off their backs.

"What compromise?"

"That's confidential."

Belmont tugged at his chains. He knew he would not be walking out of that room without the first dose of serum involved in a level-eight reassignment. The procedure was classified, but he made sure he knew about every damn thing the agency did. He knew the ins and outs of every procedure in the arsenal as well as every weapon and agent because he found the old adage the truest of them all —knowledge was fucking power.

Belmont ran a ghost organization that mirrored the agency. He was damn-sure happy that Maggie had been able to tap into every resource of his group to find him. That was why he'd recruited her. She had always been the sharpest tool in the kit.

Belmont knew chips would be put into his brain to change his identity. He also learned that the only way to beat the full immersion into another identity and be able to find his way back to himself was to hide memories by tricking his brain. He had to constantly tell himself that Daisy and Ed didn't exist so if he saw them while he was the other person, he wouldn't have an emotional reaction strong enough to activate the connective chip and stop his heart instantly.

He had never been so fucking insulted and demeaned by the agency. He'd been their top security agent even though he wasn't active. He couldn't stop wondering why in the hell they were decommissioning him. He hadn't compromised an international mission or the agency. He hadn't betrayed his oath. As he lay on the table undergoing the full procedure of losing himself, he vowed to find answers and make whoever was behind this pay.

When Maggie and Grey gave Belmont the rundown report of what had happened to him, he learned two things. First, it had been a concerted effort between holdout shareholders from the days of Lord & Lord Steel—his father's company—and senior agents within the agency to take over his enterprise. Secondly, once the takeover was finished, they were planning on killing Meyer Schulz. Grey had discovered the code red in Meyer Schulz's file. Once the company was in the hands of the usurpers, they never wanted Belmont Lord to rise again. Not only that, but they planned to kill Daisy and Ed too.

Belmont squeezed his eyes shut as he waited for the anger to subside. To imagine his beautiful wife and child's lives snuffed out because of greed made his blood boil hotter than lava. No way. The time had come for his shadow organization to put an end to the agency. They had crossed the line and were at the point of no return.

Beck plucked another one of Belmont's hairs from his beard. "We're done."

Belmont stood up from the metal chair that had been brought in by the forensics team. His glare rolled around the room. He couldn't remember one iota of what he had gone through when he was living in the cramped space for nearly a year. He could guess, though. The agency had used him as their personal angel of death. Belmont's team had been working around the clock, covertly compiling data about all of Meyer Schulz's assignments from the agency's mainframe. He hadn't received the complete report as of yet. He was sure that Meyer hadn't operated in the same confines as Red Cloud did, with killing being the last resort.

A prep team was finishing up preparing the cabin for the media frenzy that was to soon descend on it. They had twenty-four hours to offload and install steel beams, which were flown in by helicopter. The beams were to be erected along the walls of the cabin to make it appear as if Belmont was held captive in a prison he could not escape. None of the materials used in the renovation were new. Belmont was there to leave fingerprints and other trace evidence on the new additions. The team also had to make it look as though other than Belmont, only a ten-man rescue crew had set foot on the property in the last three days. They had to be very meticulous regarding what type of boot left prints in the soft soil and tracked debris into the cabin. As far as the front entrance went, the wooden door had to be busted and the lock blown on the bar door.

Garnering another complete look at his previous living quarters, Belmont was glad for the permanent amnesia. He'd lived like an animal who was only let out to do harm and then wrangled back into his cage.

Grey stepped up next to him. "Ready for round two?"

Belmont gulped. "Yeah."

"Then we better move out. Make sure you stay on the runner."

Belmont looked down and stepped onto the yellow vinyl. He took one step before a slot in the wall caught his attention. His mind captured a flash of a black sack on the floor beneath it. Anxiety set in. He remembered eagerly waiting for deliveries, which usually consisted of food, weapons, toiletries, and cleaning supplies. However, he specifically remembered always staring at the hatch. It was sloppily made. Sometimes the delivery person's fingers would show. Belmont liked those moments because they made him feel he was not alone, even if the delivery person's company was fleeting. He searched deep within himself to figure out why he'd just remembered that. Perhaps the memory had something to do with waiting for the love he had lost. The hand reminded him that he had human connections outside of the mental prison the agency had put him in.

"Beck, did anyone collect from the slot?" Belmont asked.

Beck looked to where he was pointing. "Affirmative."

"I need those results ASAP."

Once they were in the helicopter, Grey alerted his team to go public with a story of Belmont's liberation. That was going to put the heat on the agency and Lord & Lord Enterprise's board of directors. They had a small window of time to make the right people pay for what they'd done to him and his family. The second step to slicing off the head of the dragon was meeting with a few allies. He had evidence to hand over. And once the ball was rolling, that evidence would ensure Daisy's safety.

EIGHT HOURS LATER

BELMONT'S GUN SMOKED SO HOT THAT HE HAD THE goods to kill two birds with one molten bullet. Caesar Hoover and Kelly Rush, directors of top government agencies, agreed to meet with him at an undisclosed location in Maryland. The trees, dirt roads, and trail that led to another cabin brought back chilling memories. Belmont knew for sure that all kinds of top-secret shit had happened in the woods, and as Meyer Schulz, he'd been one of those clandestine matters.

The two men were already there when Belmont arrived. He carried the briefcase with everything they'd need to bring down the agency.

When the men were seated around the table, Hoover and Rush pored over the documents with a fine-toothed comb.

"Weren't you an active agent for them?" Hoover asked.

"Fifteen years ago under Thomas Wright. Back when they had a fucking conscience."

Hoover sniffed. "They were more of a help than a hindrance back then."

"What the fuck is going on here?" Rush shook a document vigorously. "They interfered with all of these investigations? Why?"

"Their interest changed from honor to profit."

Rush's grimace intensified as he kept reading.

It was time to put the final nail in the coffin. And so Belmont began to explain how the agency had never guessed that he would escape. Earlier, while searching the Alaskan cabin, Belmont's team had found external hoses that snaked through four vents. Beck identified them as Class-8 Lines, which were hoses designed to carry large doses of poisonous gas into a confined area. That proved what he already knew—they were planning on killing him. Leif Doe, one of Belmont's level-ten covert investigators, discovered a tie between the agency and the board. He couldn't contact Maggie directly because the agency was watching her every move. They knew she was operating against them and was using some pretty remarkable resources, which they tried to uncover with no luck. But Leif was able to slip a message directly to Daisy, whom the agency had become sloppy about watching. Leif used Irwin, the driver, who was a level-two agent for Belmont's security company, to keep tabs on Daisy's comings and goings. On the morning she asked Irwin to take her to the address, Leif called Laura Altman, using voice modulation to sound like Stacy Pruitt, and said that they had a big problem and should meet that morning at their usual place. He did the same with Stacy. And when the women dialed the secure line to confirm the interaction, Leif was able to direct their calls to him. It worked perfectly. Daisy reported back to Maggie, who then knew which road to take in order to find out what had happened to Belmont.

The week before, Belmont's covert operators had worked overtime trying to learn the identity of the new head of the agency. Not many people knew Thomas Wright was the previous director of the agency. It was the sort of information that stayed secret so their enemies couldn't cut off the head and thereby kill the body. But two days earlier, Belmont's team discovered the name of the current director. Belmont wasn't surprised. With the director's identity now known, Grey was also able to follow a lead to a pot of gold covered in shit.

Belmont played the audio, and Hoover and Rush listened as the board and the current director, Harold Doe, were listening in on a live recording of Belmont's abduction up until the point where Natasha confirmed that he had been contained.

"Well, I'll be damned," Hoover said after the recording ended.

"It was stupid for Harold to be there, but fortunately for us, he prefers to be hands-on. It's his ego." Belmont dropped another load of documents on the security directors, including a list of calls made by Harold Doe in security-zone hot spots.

"You mean we got this fucker on tape?" Rush asked.

Belmont gave both men a flash drive. "This investigation can't drag on. You know what's at stake."

"As long as all of this checks out, we'll make arrests within forty-eight hours."

"And keep it contained. You have some security breaches within your divisions."

Hoover grimaced. "Care to share?"

Belmont issued the last and final document for them, which included a list of double agents.

"Which one of you would like to make the arrest on Harold Doe, real name Timothy Bass? I've got him cornered."

Hoover and Rush looked at each other as though they couldn't believe their luck.

"I will," Hoover said.

"Looks like I should," Rush said at the same time.

"His crimes are national and international. Teaming up makes a bigger impact. Plus, there are twenty-six other arrests to be made," Belmont said.

"Makes sense to me," Rush said.

Hoover nodded once in agreement.

"Look forward to a call from my cousin, Maggie Adams. She'll feed you Harold Doe's location. She can subdue him if you like, but I think you'll want your people to do that."

Hoover sniffed. "I've been trying to convince Adams to join our team."

Belmont threw his hands up jokingly. "Hey, don't try to poach my people."

Both men chuckled. Despite Hoover's statement, Belmont understood that they knew Maggie would be more of a benefit to them operating in secrecy.

Rush looked at Belmont. "So, Red Cloud, who else did you send a recording of the meeting to?"

"Only you."

"Is this a gift or an exchange?" Hoover asked.

Belmont grinned. There was a rule around those parts that no one got something for nothing. And it was time to let them know what he wanted for this information he'd dropped in their laps.

SIXTEEN HOURS LATER

A FORMAL INVITATION WAS SENT TO ALL FIVE shareholders regarding Jack Lord's status. The final verdict was that Jack Lord had lost most of his brain functions and, despite aggressive treatment, hadn't recovered, so he was willing to sell his shares in Lord & Lord Enterprises. They were to meet that day in order to discuss how to move forward.

So as all five shareholders sat in the conference room, conversation resonated as a buzz of excitement—at least until Jack Lord himself, strong, confident, and with his faculties clearly intact, strolled in followed by Fred, Gabe, and Jetson Gordon, whom he'd never met until that day. The shareholders' shocked gazes bounced from face to face. Belmont had to admit that he'd received the moment of satisfaction he'd been seeking.

William Carlyle was sitting at the head of the table, perhaps because he owned the most shares. Belmont walked up to him.

"Remove yourself, please," he said, glaring at the man.

Carlyle loosened his tie as he stood. Once the seat was clear and Carlyle was sitting elsewhere, Belmont spoke. "First order of business: check your cellular devices."

He waited until they had done what he said. It had been a long time since he'd been in a room with William Carlyle, Theodore Hughie, Griswold Holt, Maxwell Benedict, and Sid Gottfried. None of them were under the age of sixty-five. They had gray hair and old money, which had never been able to buy them the controlling interest in Lord & Lord Steel. Belmont thought they were behind the airplane crash that had killed his parents. He had evidence, and that day, he was using it to end their affiliation with his company.

Sid Gottfried was still trying desperately to power his device. "Won't work. Your devices have been turned off remotely. I won't grandstand, even though you had me kidnapped and planned to murder my family and me after you got your hands on our company." Jack's glare rolled around the table. "Count your blessings that you're still breathing."

Griswold Holt straightened his husky form and stretched his neck. "What the hell are you talking about, kid?"

Belmont sniffed bitterly. Referring to him as a kid was their fucking default. Their lack of respect for him as a man and a formidable foe had always been their weakness. He gestured toward Fred, who opened his laptop and played the recording from the meeting they'd held the day he was coerced into driving off with Natasha on the threat that his family would be killed. The men remained stone faced.

Belmont smirked. "Do you think this doesn't touch you?"

"I see we have nothing more to discuss here."

Griswold Holt pushed his chair back, getting ready to stand.

"Keep your ass in that chair," Belmont growled.

Holt froze.

"None of you were physically in the room, but you were on the call. Titan's conference call, pin number 6324."

Belmont relished in the energy that filled the room—a feeling of confusion, self-preservation, and intrigue. Since he had them where he wanted them, it was time to lower the second boom.

He nodded at Fred, who played a second recording of William Carlyle, Richard Wasserman—a board member—and Max Benedict discussing ways to undermine Belmont's jet with a guy named Lynx, who was a professional mechanical saboteur. It was Belmont who'd planted the wire on Lynx. After it was clear his parents' jet had been tampered with, he set out to look for answers. The agency couldn't give him any real assistance in matters that didn't directly relate to their interests, so he recruited a hacker named Grey Lansing that he met through another hacker named Presley Choice, who swore Grey was the best there was. Presley was right —Grey was the best, and it was easy for him to discover the tie between the shareholders and Lynx.

Belmont could've threatened Lynx, but he didn't. Instead, he worked behind the scenes, first hacking the bank accounts and email accounts of all the shareholders. He learned who were friends and who were foes and which ones were willing to sell their interest in his father's company at a premium price. Belmont's father, Charles Edward Lord, had owned one percent of Lord Steel. But when he needed more money to expand, he sold private shares but at no more than five percent per shareholder, with him maintaining fifty-five percent controlling interest. Belmont and Charlie inherited their father's stake in the company. And with their father gone due to foul play, Belmont wanted all shareholders gone. Most of the shareholders didn't want to sell, even those who were strapped for cash, but Belmont went to step two—using their secrets against them. And after coercing them to sell, he offered them a lower price per share than he would've if they hadn't made him work so hard to comply. So at the end of Belmont's push to become sole owner of his father's enterprise, he had a whopping seventy-five percent stake in the company.

But the five men left, the ones Belmont glared at as he played the audio of them paying someone to sabotage his airplane, never stopped wanting it all.

"It won't be so simple. Not like it was with the father—what was his name?" Lynx's recorded voice said.

"Charles Lord, and do whatever you have to do to bring this joker's airplane to the ground," Griswold said.

"How soon?" Lynx asked.

"As soon as yesterday," Theodore Hughie says.

Belmont nodded, and Fred closed his laptop. The shareholders were all at a loss for words. Some of them quickly looked toward the door, probably contemplating an escape but realizing they had nowhere to run to.

"The first recording has been turned over to the appropriate authorities. Your board members may be in trouble, but I haven't exposed evidence of your involvement in that meeting—not yet." Belmont cracked a tiny smile. He had never taken so much pleasure in having his enemies trapped in checkmate. "Kidnapping, industrial espionage, and conspiracy to commit murder, and all of it provable." Belmont nodded at Fred and Gabe. One started at one end of the table and the other at the opposite end, passing out contracts and stock sale-and-purchase agreements.

"What do you want, Jack?" William Carlyle asked.

"You know what I want. I want you and your board members out of my fucking company."

"This is robbery," Theodore Hughie said, reading the per-share price.

Belmont nodded. "Yes. It is."

The men looked around the table at each other.

"What's our guarantee?" Carlyle asked.

"My word is your guarantee. You have right here and right now to make your decisions. If one of you refuses, then all of you will be facing arrest before you step out of this building."

They knew he did not make empty threats. Belmont stood, and Fred, Gabe, and Jet followed suit.

"I'll give you five minutes to discuss this among yourselves. Be careful. What you say can be used against you in a court of law."

The four men filed out of the room. Gabe and Fred went to the legal department to get ready to electronically file the agreements. Instead of hanging around outside the door, Belmont waited in his office with Jet, who lately had taken the room over as his own. Belmont could smell Daisy's scent the moment he walked inside. He could also detect that look in Jet's eyes. Dexter Frampton had worn that same look.

Out of respect for Jet, Belmont took the seat opposite the big chair. "My wife left quite an impression on you."

Jet hesitated, looking uncertainly at the executive's seat.

"Please. Sit," Belmont said, making a point of speaking in a more inviting tone than the one he'd used with the shareholders.

Jet sat awkwardly. "She's a beautiful woman. Smart too. Extremely intelligent."

Belmont grinned from ear to ear. "That's why I left her in charge. She's pragmatic and able to listen to those who have answers to things she doesn't know about. I married way above my pay grade."

Jet shrugged his forehead. "She's above all of our pay grades."

The two men chuckled.

"In all seriousness, I want to commend you for handling the issue with the contracts," Belmont said.

"Again, Daisy's the one who brought it to my attention, and we figured out together who might have been at fault."

Belmont was now fully appreciative of the way Jet revered his wife. He'd been really jealous when Daisy got close to Dexter Frampton, but they'd worked on their relationship after that, and he was no longer threatened by the fact that other men found his wife irresistible.

"You continued with the probes, and I was told you let go of Waite Miller, Kirk Williams, Janet Stanley, Ken Pritchett, and Tom Beard."

"Those are the ones I had the strongest proof against."

Belmont nodded. There were a few more project managers who were lying low. He planned to go where they were hiding and fire their asses as well. However, he admired Jet's work and had a proposition for him. "How would you like to stay on as president of Lord & Lord Enterprises?"

Jet sat back in his seat as if propelled by excitement. He rounded his shoulders and sat up straight. "Um, sure. Um, yes. I'm sure we can work something out."

Belmont held out his hand, and Jet shook it.

There were three knocks on the door, and Fred stuck his head inside. "Their five minutes are up."

CHAPTER NINETEEN

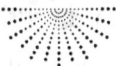

ONE DAY EARLIER

"Wow. Well, congratulations. Thanks for inviting me, but..." I look around my office. I've been stuck in this apartment for over a week, and it's starting to get to me. "You know what? I'll be there."

Robert gives me the address and time of the spur-of-the-moment wedding ceremony between him and Carter. He also reminds me that there's no reception. After he and Carter take their vows, they're flying to Bora Bora.

"So why so sudden, if you don't mind asking?"

"Planning, invitations, and all that shit was getting in the way. All we want is to be married and for the people we like to be there."

I chuckle. "I understand. And I'm glad you like us."

He laughs. "We definitely do. What about Jack? How's he doing?"

His question sucks the joviality right out of our conversation. I haven't heard from Belmont since the day he kissed me and waltzed out of our apartment. I don't know if he's dead or alive. I haven't heard a peep from Maggie, either. But I'm not sure how to answer correctly.

"He's well," I say in a manufactured optimistic tone.

"Are you still sitting in the driver's seat at Lord & Lord?"

"Um, no. Jetson Gordon has taken over."

"Then he's the one that initiated the mass firings, or was it Jack?"

I feel as if Robert is fishing. But we're friends, so I explain the contract situation to him.

"Well, I'll be damned. They tried to sink the ship from the inside," he says.

"It was your contract that started the investigation."

"I haven't been at the center of a shit storm in ages." Leave it to Robert Tango to keep the heaviness out of a conversation.

We laugh, but Robert has to go soon after. After we hang up, I go about my day as usual. However, Ed and I had spent so much time together, he needed a break from me. So he started spending a couple of hours in the afternoon with his DVDs—*The Red Planet Adventure*, *Hanging With Number One*, and of course, *Barney*. When he's done, I let him play on his keyboard in my office. I'm back to working with my bakeries again. I really love it, and boy, did I miss it. Ed also likes spending time in the kitchen while Dallas and I prepare new items for the menu. Dallas is definitely the best cook Belmont's ever employed, and his pastries and meals are mouth-watering perfection.

Tonight after dinner, Ed and I do numbers-and-letters apps on the computer. I finally finish reading *Peter Pan* to him, and he goes to bed.

Before I go to bed, I call Susan to see if she's still in the city. To my surprise, she is.

"So what's the scope of the relationship between you and Fred?" I ask.

Although I can't see her, I can feel her grinning. "We're two adults who like each other a lot."

"And?" I'm grinning too.

"And we're dating."

"And living together?"

Susan laughs. "I'm only staying with him while I visit the city."

"Well, you've been visiting the city for ten months."

"Actually..." she says as if she's about to disclose the most amazing information ever.

She goes on to tell me that she and Fred are taking a trip to the Maldives next week and then leaving from there to Iceland. Every second she spends with him has been the time of her life, whether they're watching a movie together, having long conversations about the state of the universe, or yes, even making love.

"He's exciting," she emphatically says. "He's taken me to parts of this city I didn't know existed. We've danced burlesque, boogied disco style, and even had our own private performance of *Romeo and Juliet*! And then he's smart too."

I'm waiting for her to pause and take a break, but now she's gushing about Fred's level of intelligence. Then she goes on about his family. His mother is still alive, and she's ninety-six and as happy and healthy as a lark. She lives in Connecticut, and they're driving out to see her next week.

Finally, she catches her breath. "But enough about me. How are you?"

With all her big-time plans, I'm a little hesitant to ask her to babysit Ed tomorrow. I feel as if she's drifted toward having the time of her life, and that means far away from being my full-time babysitter. Heck, she's been my nanny, and I haven't had to pay her a dime.

"I'm fine," I say. "Robert Tango invited me to his surprise wedding tomorrow evening. I'm not sure if I can go, but..."

"Yes."

"Huh?"

"I'll be over tomorrow to babysit. I've been missing Ed to death. Is he still playing his piano?"

I smile, just picturing him judiciously tapping out sounds on his keyboard. "Every day!"

Susan goes on about all the schools for geniuses that Fred said would be good for a child like Ed. Do I gush about Belmont like this? I don't think so. Another thirty minutes course by before I tell her I absolutely have to go to bed.

Susan laughs. "Look at me going on and on. How about I come over around noon?"

"That'll be perfect."

I LOOK UP AT THE TALL BUILDINGS TO THE EAST AND west of ours. I'm a little skittish, wondering if a sniper is positioned and ready to gun me down or something. The two security guards walked me all the way to the car. They tried to stop me from leaving until one of them made a call. I asked if that was Belmont he was speaking to, and he shook his head. After two minutes exactly, he nodded at the other security person and asked if they could escort me to my car.

Perhaps the situation has cooled down. Maybe Belmont will be home soon.

"Good afternoon, Daisy," Irwin says.

I wonder if he knows that I know he's part of Belmont's secret security team. I choose not to divulge that piece of information. "Good afternoon."

"To Teterboro?"

"Yes."

The car pulls away from the curb. It feels good to get moving again. It also felt good to put on a slinky black cocktail dress with my long, tailored black cashmere coat. I straightened and used a curling iron to curl my hair and put on makeup. I wanted to be a beautiful adult again. The last look I took in the mirror showed that I had succeeded.

The flight takes less than half an hour. Irwin

boards the flight with me so that he can drive me to the event after we land. He's never done that before, but I figure taking him on the flight is a pretty doable compromise between going alone and staying home.

Robert and Carter's ceremony is taking place at an old and beautiful chapel, which has been erected at the edge of the lake. It's nighttime, so a haze of white light rises above the grass, and special effects make the lake look as if it's glowing blue. The scenery is so dreamy that my heart flutters as I stand here taking it in.

"Daisy Lord!" a woman calls excitedly from the distance.

I whip myself around to see who said that. My smile broadens at the sight of Monroe, wrapped in a red satiny ankle-length trench coat and slinky high heels, skipping in my direction. Then my hand flies to my chest as none other than Javar Les catches up to her and puts his arm around her waist.

"Long time happy to see," Monroe says as we hug.

"You look fantastic and happy," I say.

I set my curious and shocked gaze on Javar's face. "Wow, fancy seeing you."

He gives me a careful side hug. I like it. It's never been Javar's style to worry about offending the woman he's with, but apparently, he cares enough about Monroe to be respectful of her.

"Good seeing you too," he says.

My finger shuffles between the two of them. "So you're a couple?"

"Yep. Indeed we are!" Monroe says.

"Wow."

"I know. We're like kryptonite and dynamite, but we're so far from exploding."

They gaze into each other's eyes, grinning giddily.

Javar guides her into his arms. "We're going to grow fat together—you watch."

Monroe touches my hand. "He says that because we've been eating like crazy. This is what happens when you're involved with a foodie. Did you know he was a foodie?"

I'm so delighted to see them this comfortable with each other. I shake my head. "No, I didn't."

The church bell tolls.

"We better get inside," I say.

Monroe looks up and down the walk. "Where's Jack?"

"Monroe! Daisy," Hannah calls before I can answer. Here she comes, trotting in our direction.

She hugs Monroe first and then me. She also has a guy to introduce. His name is Matt Franks.

"So Matt, you came?" Monroe asks.

"She's old news to him, Roe. I'm new news," Hannah says defensively.

I frown, confused. "News to who?"

"Oh," Monroe says as if she's about to spill the secret of the century. "You don't know, do you, Dais?"

Hannah grunts and rolls her eyes. "Matt is Carter's ex." I think she says it just to steal the satisfaction from Monroe. I see the two of them are still bickering like prickly sisters.

The bell tolls again.

"Let's just get our asses inside already," Monroe says.

We head inside. The church is lit by candles in glass sconces along the wall and the dim crystal chandeliers hanging from the rafters. The mood is warm and cozy, and so is the temperature. There are about fifty people here so far, including Vince's mother and sisters. They are Robert's family too.

"Where's Maggie?" Hannah says.

I'm facing away from her, but just before I turn to address her, in walk Maggie and Vince, holding hands. My heart stops. She's here and safe.

"I'll be back," I say to Hannah and practically leap to my feet to get to Maggie.

I say "excuse me" to every seated person I have to pass along the way. As soon as I clear the pew, the next person who walks inside the chapel makes me freeze in place. The organ starts playing as Belmont and I lock eyes. How did the organist know to add music to this moment? I'm so filled with joy that tears stream from my eyes. Someone behind me whispers, "There's Jack Lord," as my husband walks in my direction. I'm still frozen. When he wraps his arms around me and kisses my lips, I feel as if I've died and gone to Heaven.

THE CEREMONY WAS BEAUTIFUL. VINCE WAS ROBERT'S best man. After Carter and Robert said their vows and were pronounced man and wife, we joined them for fireworks and a dancing water show in the lake, which we watched from the lawn. Belmont and I couldn't stop kissing. We impatiently waited for Robert and Carter to tell us thanks for coming and give us hugs. As soon as the cordiality was over, Belmont and I escaped to our car, kissing in the backseat the entire way to the airport.

Now we're lying together on the bed in his jet. We've already made love, and connecting with his body and soul again felt so good. I'm on top of him, and his hands massage my butt. He just came after I climaxed, and he's still inside me.

"I love you." He kisses me deeply.

Dear God, I feel as if my heart may burst. "I love you too," I breathlessly say after his mouth releases mine.

Belmont groans with pleasure and thrusts my lower half against his cock. He wants to rise again, but he came so hard I'm pretty sure it's going to take him at least another hour to start round two.

"By the way, look." I show him the ring on my finger, which he bought for me last Christmas. "Remember this?"

"Hot damn." He holds my finger. "I do. Don't tell me..."

"Yes. The elves, Santa, all of it."

"Oh, babe, I'm sorry." He kisses the ring. "I see you didn't have them all thrown out on their asses."

I chuckle. "I passed out." I frown squeamishly.

"Aw, shit." Belmont flips me onto my back and tongues me deeply again. His warm and wet mouth journeys down the side of my neck, sucks and bites my left nipple, and pelts kisses down my sternum.

He sinks his tongue into my belly button before arriving at the final destination, where his tongue strokes my clit. I grasp the sheets on this bed as he makes me feel it deep within my vagina. Gosh, I missed this kind of pleasure. I'm so excited that I come fast, screaming at the top of my lungs as I quake. After my release, Belmont embraces me, holding me tight.

"I'm never going to let you go," he whispers in my ear.

I fall deeper against his body. "Promise?"

"Promise."

IT'S CHRISTMAS, AND WE'RE ALL IN BORDEAUX FOR Jacques and Madeleine's wedding. They decided to have it today instead of on New Year's. I think it has something to do with Belmont being back. The day was so unhappy for us last year when he was missing.

Ever since Belmont stuck it to his shareholders and board of directors and safely integrated himself back into our lives, Charlie calls him just about every day. The ceremony is taking place in the atrium of the castle here at Mes Fleurs Vineyard. It's a pretty simple ceremony, but there's a giant tent out on the front lawn, where a monumental reception is planned. There are about a hundred people here, and all of us are family. Everyone's standing around Jacques and Madeleine as the minister recites the customary marriage words in French.

I study all the faces. My father's brothers—Cyprus, Pey, and Dongo—are here along with their wives, children, and grandchildren. My cousin Anton, his brothers Jon Luc and Leon, sister Annabelle, and mother, Adélie, are here with their partners and kids. Actually, my aunt Lorraine, who I didn't know was Madame Josephine Beauchamp's sister, is here. My parents, Heloise, and stepfather—Joseph—are here with my half sisters Daphne and Hannah, who I'm still not very close to because of our age difference, but I love them very much. Then there are my brothers, Randall and Joseph, from my father's second marriage with Shelly Price, who decided watching Jacques get married for the third time was not her cup of tea. My mother's parents are here. Belmont and I are having dinner with them tomorrow night. I have more cousins here than I can count. I used to run away from family, but I'm excited about getting to know them all.

I smile up at Belmont, who's already watching

me with a smile. I love him so much. I also realize that this moment probably would've never been possible if our Martha's Vineyard love story hadn't happened. Out of our love came a Manhattan love story with Vince and Maggie and an LA love story with Charlie and Angel, and actually, Belmont and I can take credit for the San Francisco love story between Robert and Carter too. Our relationships all connect. I even heard Monroe and Javar are not only pregnant but also engaged. We can take credit for them too!

Belmont and I are also pregnant again. I rest my face against his chest, and he kisses the top of my head as my dad says that he takes Madeleine to be his lawfully wedded wife. Belmont doesn't know we're having another baby. I'll tell him tonight before he undresses me and makes beautiful love to me and holds me close until the sun rises, and we'll have and hold each other for another day of pure bliss.

CONTEMPORARY ROMANCE SERIES

The Dark Billionaire Jasper Christmas Trilogy

Intrigued

Desire

Claimed

The Freed Billionaire Spencer Christmas Trilogy

Enthrall

Impulse

Bliss

CONTEMPORARY ROMANCE

LOVE in the USA (The Hesters)

Once Friends **(A Hollywood Love Story) Sonja & Jay #1**

Now Lovers **(A Hollywood Love Story) Sonja & Jay #2**

Taming The Shrewd **(Another Hollywood Love Story) Elaine & Zach**

Waiting on You **(A Brooklyn Love Story) Robin & Dexter**

ABOUT THE AUTHOR

Z.L. Arkadie has been an author since July 2011, debuting with her Parched series. She has been a best-selling author in the iBooks store, holding the top spot for two weeks with her LOVE in the USA, series, which is still her most popular series to date. Currently she has written 40 novels and counting, which span over 7 series. She enjoys merging erotic romance with a solid mystery. Her favorite characters to write are sexy, strong and brooding men who find love with beautiful, independent and smart women.

When she's not writing, she loves to cook and read good books, which have the power to take her somewhere she's never been.

For more information:
zlarkadiebooks.com
contact@zlarkadiebooks.com